THE LAKE HOUSE

Cheryl Barton

Published by: Cheryl Barton Publishing, LLC

Cheryl Barton Publishing, LLC
P.O. Box 962
Reisterstown, Maryland 21136
www.crbarton.com

Ordering Information:
Quantity sales. Special discounts are available on quantity purchases by corporations, associations, and others. For details, contact the publisher at the address above.

Orders by U.S. trade bookstores and wholesalers.
Please contact prez@crbarton.com

ISBN-13: 978-1948950039
ISBN: 1948950030

Acknowledgements

I'm thankful for readers of romance who continue to stoke and inspire an author's creative ability. We are because of you.

Thank you!

Cheryl

1

Gannon Wilcox looked down at the worn, brown vintage leather pilot briefcase that sat on the floor next to his brand new brown leather canvas military sea bag. Between the two bags, he had enough clothing to last him two weeks. He wasn't concerned because if he chose to stay away longer, he was only a few hours away and could come back home to get more.

Looking around his rustic themed living space, he spotted his favorite picture of him and his dad from when he was a boy and they enjoyed fishing up at their lake house, a place his family loved going to in order to escape life's busy road.

A myriad of wonderful memories came to mind as he walked over and grabbed the picture, looking at it as if his father would suddenly leap out of the picture frame and appear in person in front of him. If he could will that to happen, he'd do it in a minute. If only there had been more time.

Gannon's heart hurt knowing that wasn't possible. A year had gone by since he, his mother and two sisters said their final farewell to the patriarch of their family who had battled a vigorous fight with cancer. With his father finally at rest and no longer in pain, he carried the weight of the times his father will miss enjoying grandchildren and long days and nights with their mother sitting on the deck at their lake house looking out over the lake that meant so much to them all.

The lake house was where he was headed for the next several weeks. No one in his family had been to the lake house since his father's passing and it was time he went there, got in a little fishing and some much-needed rest and relaxation. The plan was to have a cleaning service come in and clean the house from top to bottom and have a landscaper freshen up the surrounding property since no one had tended to it in over a year. This was the first year that no one took the time to make sure the property was being kept up. He imagined the grass was as tall as his six-foot five height, though he knew he was exaggerating the height of the foliage. He imagined the wood deck would need staining and he was positive the family's yacht Luhrs 38 Convertible boat would need to be looked at before bringing it back to the lake from where it was dry-rack stored for the year they stayed away. That boat was his father's pride and joy and he would forever make sure that it remained in pristine shape. The, Anna-Marie, the boat his father named after his mother, was a beauty in all white with red lettering on the side. The inside cabin area slept two and they even kept a small microwave and refrigerator inside. His father loved going out on the lake in the boat with their mother and times when they couldn't tear themselves away, they would sleep on it right on the lake. He smiled when he thought about the love his parents shared, something not a lot of people got to experience.

Looking around his house, he tried to remember everything he wanted to take with him. Though he initially promised himself that he would not do any work while taking this respite, he was bringing along his laptop to stay connected to the office. He'd been busy, along with his sisters, keeping the family's baby food business up and running in the past two years at the start of their father's illness. The time seemed to fly by and it wasn't until recently that he realized he hadn't taken one single day off.

Gannon was excited about going up to the cabin. For a year, he hadn't been able to take the drive to the place that his father loved going to the most. With a successful business, his father would have been able to do whatever he wanted and gone to any exotic place in the world, but whenever he wanted time off away from the office, he went straight to the lake house where he fished and spent time on his last big purchase, the Anna-Marie. With time on his hands now, Gannon was looking forward to taking the boat out on the waters beyond the lake and remembering fun times spent with this whole family on it.

With the back of his truck full of all of the food essentials he would need, he grabbed his last two bags and was almost out of the door when his cell phone rang. He had no doubt about who was calling. It had to be one of two of his pesky older sisters checking to see if he was still okay going to the cabin alone. There were so many memories there, that his sisters said they needed more time before they went. Gannon knew he was more than ready. He needed to celebrate time spent with his father.

"One more second and I would have been in my truck. What's up Dawn?" he asked. He heard her huff on the other end.

"How did you know it was me? I'm calling from Kris' phone?" Dawn said.

Gannon laughed because he knew his sisters better than they knew themselves.

"Though Kris worries about me, you're insanely worried about me all the time and I knew you wouldn't let me get up to the lake without checking in a million times," he said.

"I know and I am worried. It's been a year since dad died and we've all avoided the lake because it was his favorite place. You're going up there to spend a few weeks alone with those memories and yes, again, I was worried about you," she explained.

Gannon and his sisters were close and when one hurt, the others hurt, but he wasn't hurting as much as he had many months ago. Nothing could match the hurt of watching his father suffer through treatment and then waste away to a shell of the man he once was. He would love to have his father back, but he was glad that he no longer had to endure the kind of pain that made him want to leave.

"I told you both over dinner the other night that I'm fine. There is nothing to worry about."

"Yeah, well, I was checking to be sure. Your ex-wife stopped by the office today."

An image of Michelle, the woman whom he'd finally filed for divorce from and happily signed the last papers eight months ago. They'd had no communication since and he couldn't imagine what she wanted to talk about if she came by to see him.

"Who did she come to see?" he asked, hoping it wasn't him. He knew the obvious choice was him because his family had never really warmed up to her, so she wouldn't stop by to see either of his sisters.

"She was hoping to catch you. I told her you had taken off for a few weeks and she thought I was lying. We almost ended up in a spat until Kris came out and played peacekeeper. Imagine her thinking I would play along with some foolishness."

Gannon chuckled. They may not like his ex-wife, but Michelle sure did know Dawn.

"I'm sure she said that because during the last months of the divorce proceedings, I was at the office day and night. I was consumed with work and you know that yourself. I was doing everything to keep my mind off of my divorce and our father being gone. She probably assumed I would be there," he explained.

"She needs to go and stay away. She brought you nothing but misery."

"I know, I know. Don't get all worked up over her visit. I'll give her a call in a few days and find out what she wants. It's probably nothing, which is what she got in the divorce. I think she thought she'd get more because of the company. Either way, don't dwell on it," he said.

"Okay. I'm glad you're taking this time off because you need it. Pop getting sick and passing the torch to you to run things was major and you had a lot to learn in a short period of time. You're doing a great job, in case I haven't said it lately. The company is growing due to your new ideas and the new technology that dad wasn't willing to hear or learn about."

"It was time for a change if we were going to continue to compete with other companies. We had to step up our game. What did Michelle finally say or do?" he asked. The last thing he wanted was for her to show up at the cabin ruining his peaceful time off.

"Kris told her that you really were off and without hesitation, she believed her. Why did you ever marry that woman? I can't imagine what you saw in her other than she's drop dead gorgeous, but she's not the only pretty face out here. She sure is dumb as a bag of rocks!" Dawn said and laughed.

Gannon had to stifle his own laugh. Dawn was never one to hold back her honest opinion of anyone.

"That's not nice. I know you didn't like her, but name calling?"

Dawn laughed some more and he waited.

"Okay, you're right and I'm sorry. I should do better for someone who's thirty-one years old."

"Right, now can I leave, please?" Gannon asked while locking up his house.

"Who's keeping an eye on your house while you're away? I know you're not going to drive that long six-hour drive back from North Carolina to Georgia just to check on it."

"Russ is going to check on it and I have my mail forwarded to my assistant until I return. She'll alert me to anything important. You and Kris both have keys and I'm sure you're dying for me to tell you that you can come by and check up on my house while I'm gone. Do not raid my cabinets and blast hip-hop music. I know you love that stuff!" he expressed. Russ was a friend from their youth that he'd remain good friends with. He trusted Russ as he would a sibling.

"I promise I won't play it loud, but you know I'm going to play it some. What kind of condition do you think the lake house is in? No one has been there in over a year," Dawn said.

Gannon had been thinking the same thing before she called, but he would deal with it when he got there. Since they owned their lake house, the homeowner association fees would have covered all of the maintenance of the property in the front that was visible to traffic going by. It was the rear of the property that each owner had to maintain. With the summer crowd coming up soon, they'll be lots of businesses looking to provide that service.

"I'll deal with the grass and other landscaping. You know how mom loves all those flowers. The house needs to be cleaned and of course I want to have the boat brought up which means it needs to be cleaned and serviced. I'll also need to get the pool cleaned and filled, too," he explained. It seemed like a lot, but he was excited about being there.

"Sounds to me like you're planning on being there for longer than a few weeks, little brother," Dawn exclaimed.

"Stop calling me little brother. You're only two years older than me and a few weeks will be enough. If not, you and Kris can keep things running. I'm the only one without kids and a significant other, so I can be away. Call me if you need anything."

"I may call and come visit to get away from my hubby and the kids. I need a break, too."

Gannon laughed out loud.

"Don't even think about it. I'll talk to you in a few days and tell Kris I said don't call me every day. You'll have your hands full looking after mom. Make sure she stays busy."

Gannon knew his mother was still dealing with the loss of her husband of over forty years. They all had to deal with what was their new normal, especially her.

2

Danielle Fenton paced in frustration at herself for once again allowing her husband, rather her ex-husband, to rattle her cage. She was a glutton for punishment every time she answered one of his phone calls. What she needed to do was follow her sister's advice and change her cell phone number. Her advice was on point when she said deep down, someone doesn't really want to break free if they don't fully disconnect. There was something to be said about her allowing her star of the stage ex-husband to play with her mind. She knew she was done with him after years of his lack of respect for her and their marriage. Being divorced for six months didn't keep him from constantly pressuring her about coming back to him. If she were going to do that, she never would have filed for divorced and actually follow through with it. Blain Combs was nothing if he was persistent to the point of annoyance. He should have been this persistent about honesty in their marriage, she thought.

"Blain, I have to go. My sister is waiting on me and there is nothing else to talk about," she said, trying her best not to shout. It had been a long time since they were able to have a conversation that didn't end in her shouting in frustration.

"Yes, there is. We can talk about you coming to your senses and coming back to me," he shouted.

"We're divorced. If I didn't come back to you before it was final six months ago, what makes you think I would do it now?" she asked.

"The way I see it, we're divorced and can get a fresh start at getting it right this time. You know I love you," he pleaded.

"I got it right the first time. You were the one with the issues of trust, honesty, fidelity, womanizing, shall I continue?" she asked facetiously.

"Cute. You got jokes. This is crazy, Danni. You know you love me and I'm the only guy for you. You can't top being married to Blain Combs. No man will ever compare to me. I'm sitting at the top of every music genre right now where my latest song release has been at number one for eleven weeks. I'm a star and everybody wants to be with Blain Combs and you are no exception. This is me. You can't fight all of this. Danielle Combs was somebody with me," he said sounding smug.

Danielle felt sick to her stomach. How could she have married anyone with an ego the size of a planet.

"My name is Danielle Fenton just in case you forgot I went back to my maiden name and that name has more meaning than any other I've had. You do not have a fan cheering section over here. I was your biggest supporter for the first five years of our marriage until I realized I was just another thing for you to acquire. You walked all over me and what we had. Why would any woman with any sense of self-worth go back to a man who can't find a pair of pants with a zipper that can stay up when he's around other women? You need to move on. Like you said, everyone wants you and now that you know that's not the case with me, feel free to keep it moving and stop calling me Danni, I hate that nickname you created."

"You're so sensitive about everything. You had it all with me, money, cars, vacations, a-list parties and people waiting to deliver your every need. You were living the life and it wasn't enough for you? You were richer than you will ever be in life. What are you going to do without a college degree? Not much I'm sure. You're better off being my wife," he said in a way meant to demean her.

Danielle felt the sting of his insult. Looks like he wants to play dirty, she thought. Taking a deep breath, she dug down as deep as he had.

"For starters, I'm still rich thanks to the divorce settlement and that made me richer than I have ever been because while we were married, you controlled the finances. Next, I will not miss all of that because it certainly didn't make for a happy marriage and that's what I signed up for. Finally, what I got more than anything was paternity tests, secret STD tests, women on my social media account direct messaging me with photos of you doing things you have no business doing as a married man and when I say I had enough of all that, I meant it. None of that was worth being on your arm, so thanks for making me rich, for the two houses and the two cars from the settlement. I may not be as rich as you, but I've done pretty good for a woman who only has three years of college under her belt. I have plenty of money to get my degree and then some. Now, if you're done trying to insult me and thinking that's the key to me coming back to you, you thought wrong."

Danielle could hear Blain exasperate a huge sigh on the other end of the phone. Once again, he'd gone too far and now she was boiling made and pacing back and forth at her parents' house.

"I'm sorry, Danielle. You know how defensive I get when I'm angry in order to have my way. I didn't mean anything by it."

"Sure, you did and it's your usual go-to reaction. We are done and we really have nothing to continue talking about. The divorce was final six months ago and from what I see in the media, you are enjoying the single life. You have two babies on the way, supposedly, and I recommend you focus on them."

Saying the words, she made herself shake off the

thought that he wasn't even trying to be careful.

"But.."

"Don't try it, Blain. You and I both know those tests will come back with you as the father. I've seen the videos and the texts like everyone else in the world. They were embarrassing the first time and still are and you are out of your mind if you think I would ever consider a life with you again. There is more to life than things and money, she said.

She heard Blain laugh on the other end. This was not a time for humor.

"If that's the case, then give me back my money and the things you got in the divorce settlement," he said.

"Right, they may not be important, but they are mine. Have a good life, Blain."

Danielle hung up and tried to walk back and forth to shake off the frustration.

"Blain again?"

Danielle was startled by the sudden appearance of her mother behind her. She had been so caught up in dealing with the unwanted call from her ex that she temporarily forgot she was at her parents' house and that they were home.

"Hey, Ma. Yeah, he won't stop calling with this ridiculous notion that we should get back together and try again."

"You sister gave you a simple remedy for that."

"Why should I have to change my number? Everyone knows this number for me," she tried to rationally explain and hated the words the moment they left her mouth.

Her mother walked in front of her and shook her head.

"You sound ridiculous and that's why he keeps calling you and why you keep answering. Change the number and be done. You can text your number out to everyone you want to have it. Stop being accessible," her mother said in a matter of fact kind of way.

Danielle started to tell her that even if she did that, Blain knew enough people that he would still get her number, but then she realized how stupid it sounded in her head. She was still making excuses for a man who treated her like a doormat.

"You're right. I'm going to do it today. I'm going to spend a few days at Jenna's house and then I'm going to probably fly to New York to hang out a few days with Dean."

Her mother looked at her sideways.

"Your plan is to fly back and forth across the country to go from staying with your sister and her family to your brother? What you need is time to yourself to focus on you and what your next move is going to be. You've spent too many years being arm candy for Blain and not focusing on anything for you and you think the answer is to visit your sister and her family knowing how loud and wild her house will be with her three children under six. Then your next move is to visit your brother who will spend all of your time trying to get you to escort him to the best parties in New York City because of who your ex-husband is and you will not have any peace. What are you thinking about? None of that is the answer for you. You're still not focusing on what's next."

"I know, but what else can I do? I don't know what to do next. I haven't had much time to myself like this in years. I was always on the go following behind Blain and now all I have is time."

"That means it's time for you to appreciate all of this time a little more. Why don't you take some time and spend it at the lake house? Your father and I aren't using it this summer and your sister already said she was going to sign the kids up for summer daycare in Texas where they live. You'll have the lake house to yourself the rest of the summer and by then, you should have a game plan in place for what's next. Go to school, start a business, I don't care what it is, but you've have enough time to get the wild life out of your system. You're twenty-nine years old and enough is enough."

"I'm sorry, Ma."

Her mother came close and gave her a hug.

"I didn't say those things for you to have something to apologize to me for. I said them because I want you to see that it's time for you to figure out what Danielle wants to do for Danielle and the lake is the place to go. I can't explain it, but that place has always made foggy situations clearer. Your mind is free to think openly there when you experience the beauty of the lake. I want you to think about doing that instead of flying around the country. Slow down for a change and dive into you. Your father has had someone maintaining the property and I can call a cleaning service to have the lake house cleaned and ready for you in a few days. Think about it."

Her mother was right. She had been so wrapped up in Blain's life for so long and none of that dealt with going to the lake house, a favorite place of hers growing up. Blain was always too busy to even entertain going to a place where they could escape the world. He always wanted the world to be a major part of their lives. The lake house is exactly what she needs to get away from everything and focus on the important things in life.

"I don't need to think about it. I'm going to the lake house. I've already put most of my things in storage and I have two management companies looking after the two houses I won in the divorce settlement. You're right that I need to start thinking about my next move and the lake house is the perfect quiet place to do that."

"Great. I'll make a few calls to have the house cleaned. The grounds around the outside are already kept up. You are beautiful and smart and you can do anything you want to do with your life. Figure that out and then do it. No more wasting your life on someone who doesn't love and respect you. You deserve better than that."

Danielle watched her mother walk away toward the kitchen, no doubt about to start dinner. Her parting words had her thinking. There once was someone who treated her like she deserved only the best and she walked away from him. That was her biggest regret in life.

**

"Do you think she'll be okay?"

James and Gail Fenton watched their youngest and most spirited child drive off from their suburban Georgia home to a place where they knew she would be able to deal with her past enough to move forward into her future. Her life hadn't been the easiest or the most private, but the lake house on the lake would bring it all into perspective.

James embraced her lovingly.

"She's going to be fine. If she survived being married to Blain Combs, she'll survive a few months at the lake. Going to the lake helped us through a trial or two in our marriage. We were always able to find our way by remembering what was important. By the time she leaves there, she'll have a much better understanding of herself and what her life is supposed to be."

They waved when Danielle waved to them out of the window. She was on her way to the lake house.

3

Gannon pulled into the driveway at his family's North Carolina lake house and waited a few minutes before getting out as memory after memory flooded his mind, spanning his life up until a year ago. Some of the best times of his life were spent here, especially the long summer months when, as a family, they would come up following the last day of school and he and his sisters would beg to be able to stay until the day before the first day of school at the end of the summer. He looked up and down the long row of lake front houses and remembered the fun times with all of his friends where they swam, fished, camped out and wreaked childhood madness, all in fun.

His father had their lake house built many years ago once his self-made, homemade baby food business made enough money where they could splurge. He and his sisters never wanted for anything and were taught to always appreciate everything. Their times at the lake house would never be forgotten and memories of his father would always live with him, with them all.

Peering out of the front window while sitting in the driveway in front of the two-car garage, Gannon checked out the exterior which had been pristinely maintained. With the weather warming up, flowers and bushes his mother had planted years ago were starting to spring forth. He looked at the porch that curved around the left side of the house and remembered as a child, the moment his father pulled up with everyone piled in their truck, he and his sisters would jump out, run up on the porch that took them to the back of the house. Once back there, steps led to the large back yard and then eventually to the pier where they would sit for hours overlooking the water. When he was in middle school, his father added an in-ground pool, the first of all the neighbors which made their house the place to hang out. It was during those middle school years that he'd begun to notice Danielle.

He smiled thinking about her and all of the time they spent together once they became a couple during their high school years. Looking further to the left, he looked at the house where she and her family spent their summers very close to his. He loved those times even though the plans they had to live happily ever after as husband and wife never panned out. He spent years wondering how their lives could have taken such different paths. Even now, the thought of what they shared tugged at his heart, but there was no reason to dwell on a life together that wasn't meant to be. She chose another and eventually, so did he.

Opening the garage doors, he stepped out into the hot afternoon sun. In a few short weeks, the community would be swarming with new generations of children who would grow to love the area as much as he had. With school about to be out for the year, his sister, Kris, would normally be preparing to bring her kids up for a few weeks for their summer vacation. He knew they missed being on the lake. He hoped with him coming up and helping them all get back to a normal life, she would change her mind and come back to the place that was as much of a home to them as their home in Georgia. He loved watching his niece and nephew having as much fun and making new friends as they did when they were kids. The lake house on the lake was a magical place.

Grabbing his bags from the back of his truck, he disarmed the alarm on the panel in the garage and entered the house. His first plan was to air the house out by opening all of the windows and allowing the late spring, early summer breeze flow throughout.

Entering the house through the garage, he entered the kitchen and was happy that his first call early one morning a week ago was to a local cleaning service to come and give the house a thorough cleaning. He was expecting them within the hour. Walking throughout, his heart began to beat faster as a pain flowed through it when he came across places where his father loved to sit and read the daily newspaper followed by completing the crossword puzzle. He loved doing anything that kept his mind fresh.

As he entered the family room, the center of the entire house, he looked at the line of pictures that fanned out across the mantel above the fireplace. He laughed to himself when he looked at the years of photos of funny faces, funny outfits and family fun. The pictures reflected back to their first summer at the lake until their last summer as a family before his father's illness kept them away. One of the last sets of photos were of his other sister, Dawn and her husband and son. His father had the biggest, brightest smile on his face as he nuzzled the neck of his grandson. His father loved family.

"This is the life," he said out loud.

After unlocking and raising the four large bay windows that overlooked the large deck out back and the unobscured view of the vast lake, he completed his check of the house. He walked into the dining room where they ate all of their family meals and he began pulling the covers from the furniture. When plumes of dust filled the air, he covered his mouth and nose to keep from inhaling almost two years of sediment. That was a sign of how long it had been since anyone came up to the house. He raised the eight windows in this room along the walls, four that overlooked the back of the house as they did in the family room while the other four gave a perfect view of Danielle's family home next door. He wondered if her parents still came up every summer now that their children were grown. He had fond memories of not only Danielle, but her older brother and sister, Donte and Jenna. He hadn't seen her family since his father's funeral and was happy they were able to attend along, with the exception of Danielle, who he knew, like the rest of the world, that she was hiding out after her life with her celebrity husband blew up and became fodder for all of the news outlets.

Taking the stairs that led from the dining room to the second level, he took them two at a time and opened the doors and windows in all four bedrooms, one of which was a guest room. Growing up, his parents had their room, he had his own room being the only boy and his sisters shared a room, leaving one extra room. The original thought was his sisters would each enjoy their own rooms, but they loved sharing one room during the summer. When they were home at their house in Georgia, they had separate rooms, but spent all of their time in each other's rooms. He would leave the cleaning crew to remove the rest of the coverings over the furniture seeing them in every room.

Going back downstairs, he opened the sliding glass door that led to the deck from the family room and expected to see grass overgrown and weeds that would need to be attended to. What he saw was a totally different story. The grass had recently been cut with trimmed walkways. He looked over the railing at weed-less flower beds and the two large trees that were between the house and the lake had been trimmed with branches cut back. Surprisingly, he could see new flowers had also been planted. Someone had taken care of the property in the back and he didn't know who. With a questionable look on his face, he looked down the row of houses to his left and to his right and noticed that the only houses that had been taken care of were his and the house next door, the one that belonged to the Fenton family. He wondered if her parents had seen to it knowing that his family was still reeling from their loss. He hadn't seen a car when he drove up, but with each house having either a one or two-car garage, they could be there and he wouldn't know it.

Going down the back steps, he walked toward their house hoping to catch someone in to inquire and thank them if it was them. Walking across the brick pathway that the two families agreed to add many years ago to keep the kids from running back and forth across the grass, he took them and walked up the back steps that led to their deck. Knocking lightly, he waited to see if anyone would answer. Not hearing or seeing any movement, he turned to walk back to his house when the sliding glass door opened and standing in front of him was a woman he hadn't seen since he was twenty-one-years old. Danielle.

4

"Gannon?"

He saw the same ghostly look on her face as he was sure she was seeing on his.

"Danielle? Hi," he said, completely shocked to see her after expecting either her parents or perhaps her brother or sister at the door. Never in a million years would he have expected to see her.

"Hi! What are you doing here at the lake?" she asked.

Danielle wanted to take the words back the minute she said them. It was obvious he was at the lake because his family had the house next door which meant he wanted to be there.

"Here at the lake or here at your house?" he asked and smiled.

"Well, I guess both," she said.

"I'm at the lake taking a break from work and I'm here at your house because I saw that the yard out back had been landscaped and I noticed your family's property had also been done. No one in my family did this and I wanted to say thanks if your parents were here and took care of it. I was expecting to see major work that needed to be done like the inside of the house."

"Yeah, that was my dad. He has a guy he contracted to keep both properties up this summer. He and my mom weren't sure if your family were going to use the house this year, but he wanted to be sure everything remained in tip-top shape."

"That was nice of them. Are they here?" he asked, looking beyond her.

"No, just me. They're not coming up this summer. They decided to go to Europe for a few weeks, but they may stop up for a weekend or two before the end of summer."

"Please, thank them on behalf of my family."

Danielle was trying to talk over the lump that formed in her throat. It wasn't just about the fact that she knew he was hurting over the loss of his father, but seeing him standing in front of her after many years was a shock to her system. Old feelings came back of a time when they shared words of love and on her eighteenth birthday, they shared their first sexual experience. She had been in love with Gannon Wilcox and then walked away from him thinking the grass was greener and it wasn't. She tried to shake of the onslaught of thoughts and feelings of a time in life when she was happiest being in his arms and sharing dreams for their future. Life was simpler back then on the lake.

"I will do that. It's really good to see you. It's been a lot of years," she said.

"Yes, it has and it's good to see you, too. You look as beautiful as ever," Gannon added as he slid his hands into the pockets of his jeans and rocked back and forth haphazardly. He never expected the door would open and Danielle would be on the other side. The last time he saw her, he had been home on leave during the third year of his tour in the army and surprised her at the lake where he ended up being the one surprised. He knew his family was at the lake and by way of letters and texts, he knew that Danielle was planning to visit the lake with her family that summer. She was in between semesters at school and looked forward to the break before her senior year.

When he pulled up to the house in his rental car, his sister met him at the car, completely surprised to see him. He remembered she was trying to tell him something, stumbling over her words when he told her he would be right back and ran toward Danielle's house. If he had waited a few minutes and either talked to her or went inside to say hello to his family, he would have been warned that Danielle had invited her new boyfriend, someone from her college that she had been seeing and never told him about. He was caught unaware when he went around to the back of her house and saw them sitting together hugging and kissing on her back deck. In all of their communicating as often as he could, she never told him about another guy and when she tried to explain that she wanted to tell him, but couldn't find the words, he went back to his family's house where he stayed inside the rest of the day. After staying the night, he drove from the lake back to his family's home in the suburbs of Georgia where he remained while on leave.

"Thank you," he heard her say, jogging him back to the fact that they were standing on the deck, which was also the last place he'd seen her in person years ago.

"Are you just getting here?" he asked.

"I've been here a few days. Are you staying all summer?" she asked, curious. She was trying to quickly imagine what it would be like with them being right next door to each other since she was planning on staying through the summer.

"Probably not the entire summer, but most of it. I'll need to go back to Georgia a few times to handle some in-person work things, but my plan is to stay for most of the summer and take some time to unwind and relax. I haven't been able to do that since my father passed and I took over as head of the company."

Danielle perked up. She had yet to say anything about that.

"I'm sorry about you losing your dad. I know how close the two of you were and how your family seemed like the perfect, Brady Bunch, like family," she quipped.

"Yeah, people called us that, but we had our issues like other families. Coming to the lake each year made any issues we had disappear. The good thing was the good always outweighed the bad and we knew how precious our love was as a family."

"I'm sorry I didn't make your father's services with my family. I was out of the country, but I hope you received my flowers and my note," she said.

Danielle knew her explanation was no excuse considering how close their two families had become being next to each other for over twenty years. The fact that they were a couple from age fifteen until age twenty-one when she made the worst choice of her life choosing Blain over him, would undoubtedly be uncomfortable to use as an excuse for not being supportive. They hadn't said anything to each other since then. At least he didn't turn and walk away the minute he saw her open the door. She was childish back then and now she was a woman and looking at Gannon, that young boy was gone and in place of him stood a hot, gorgeous man.

"I did, thank you and it's okay. I know you would have been there if you could have been. The services were nice and your parents, brother and sister represented your family well. They came by the house every day and your mom stayed from sun up until sundown doing everything for my mother. You know your family is my family and vice versa," he said.

"Yes. Our families have always been like that. You look great. Years have been good to you," Danielle said admiringly.

Danielle couldn't help herself when she allowed her eyes to travel all over his body, marveling at how sexy and in-shape he was. Gannon had always been handsome, but now, he far exceeded that word with his dark-brown skin, deep black eyes, neatly trimmed goatee, bald head and that deep sexy voice. Through his fitted blue t-shirt, she could see muscles for days. The man still did things to her body without even touching her.

Gannon heard a hint of flirting in her voice and definitely in the way she was looking at him. He still remembered how a simple look from her would drive him wild. Looking at her, she still had that impact.

"Thank you. Life has been good to us both, I see. Still the most beautiful girl in the world." If he meant for his words to come across as a slight flirt, he succeeded. The look on her face showed that they were equally remembering a time when they would be all over each other.

"Thank you. Through the ups and downs, life is still good," she said.

"I agree and I'm sorry to hear about your marriage not working out."

Gannon meant to toss that out there. He may be flirting a little, but there was still an elephant in the room.

"Sorry about yours, too. My mom told me the two of you split up. I guess our paths in life weren't exactly the best, huh?"

Gannon hunched his shoulders.

"It was the path we took, right? We can't knock that. Every day of life is a lesson learned and I've learned that life does go on. The world does continue to spin and waits for no one to get it right," he explained and hoped Danielle didn't read too much into his comment. He was speaking more about his own life and not hers.

"That's true."

"Well, I don't want to keep you. I'm just getting here and I'm waiting on a cleaning crew to come and give the house a major cleaning. I guess I'll be seeing you since we'll both be here."

"I guess we will. I'll be sure to relay your thanks to my dad and if you need anything, stop over anytime," Danielle said, meaning every word.

"I will do that."

Gannon turned and walked away, giving Danielle a slight wave as he hopped down the steps and jogged over to his house. The minute he was inside where no one could see him, he finally released the breath he felt like he had been holding since the moment the door opened and a woman so beautiful that he wasn't sure he wouldn't hyperventilate, stood before him like a dream.

Danielle had aged beautifully and was still as lovely as the day he first recognized she was no longer that tomboy running behind him and his friends around the lake. One summer she was in shorts, a baseball cap and sneakers and then the next, she came walking down her steps in a yellow sundress with sandals on, earrings in her ears and her hair permed and flowing down her back and around her face. She no longer wanted to run behind the boys, but preferred hanging with the other girls talking about boys and makeup. Things changed for him that day and every summer after that, until high school when he asked if he could hold her hand while they watched a movie on the big screen at the lake. Every summer the families pooled their money to provide lots of fun activities for the kids and one of those was to have a company provide a family movie night twice a month. They brought in a large truck with a huge screen, several food trucks and other activities.

For five years, they were inseparable. Luckily, during the rest of the year, the families lived only miles apart in Georgia, so they had the chance to hang out at times when they weren't at the lake. They went to each other's proms and other dances and school events. Danielle was on the cheering squad for her school and in their senior year, she became the team captain and the most popular girl at her school.

He played several sports and loved looking in the stands and seeing her sitting with his family cheering him on.

Danielle had been his biggest supporter when he chose to go into the service instead of head off to college like a lot of their friends. It was during that time that she'd found someone else and broke his heart, something that took years for him to get over. He had only planned on doing four years in the army, but instead did eight to avoid going back home and dealing with the fact that Danielle had run off and married a guy she'd met in college who ended up being one of the biggest pop singers in the country. She chased fame and found a snake in the grass. He'd kept up on her life over the years and hated seeing story after story of her husband's infidelity and overall horrible treatment of her. To Blain Combs, she was nothing more than a prized possession to walk around on his arm and parade like the star of his three-ring circus. She was worth more than that, but it took him a few years to understand the draw and he forgave her, though he'd never told her.

Thinking of their time back then, he loved her more than anything and wanted to marry her, but she had other plans he didn't know about. For that, he carelessly dated women wherever he was stationed and ended up marrying a woman who didn't want the same things he did. Now, they were both divorced and found themselves at the lake.

"It's going to be a long, hot summer," he said just as the bell rang. His cleaning crew had arrived, allowing him to think of something, anything else besides Danielle and how much he still wanted her.

5

Danielle was in her third day at the lake house and like the past two days, she sidled up to the window that faced the Wilcox house hoping to catch a glimpse of Gannon. After talking that first day, she had seen him coming and going, but they hadn't had another conversation since then. She could chalk it up to the fact that she hadn't gone out in the past few days, choosing instead to enjoy quiet time to herself like her mother suggested and it was working. The only problem is that with every waking and sleeping moment, she hadn't been able to think of much else other than him.

"Why do you have to be so sexy and virile?" she asked herself as she looked out of her window and into his across the way.

There had been a lot of activity at his house over the past few days. It was clear his family wasn't with him and so far, she'd seen a cleaning company, grocery store delivery truck and a pool company that came out to clean and fill the pool. Each time she spied, she watched him move about giving instructions and lending a hand to clean up.

Earlier, she had been walking down the steps and spotted him out of the large window midway down that overlooked the front of house. Gannon must have been out running because she caught him coming back all sweaty and glistening and to her delight, he had removed his shirt and was jogging with it in his hands. No way could she miss the chance to take in the sight of all that was gorgeously him. His herculean body was built like an in-shape boxer with muscles bulging in all the right places with powerful, well-toned legs that had her drawn to him like a moth to a flame. Without thinking, she scolded herself for licking her lips when he bent over showing his strong, alluring backside and imagined the powerful movements of it in the most intimate setting. The man was gorgeous and no longer the boy she knew years ago. He was now much more and her body hummed and sizzled looking at him.

She thought back to their younger years when they made love and remembered how attentive he was to her needs. Though they were virgins their first time together, over the last two years that they were together and were able to see each other, he had learned a lot about pleasing a woman and she remembered how delicious and sexy he made her feel whenever they were together.

Unlike her time with Blain, who spent more time making sure their sex life was about him before her, Gannon hadn't done that and he was a lot younger then when a lot of young guys were only thinking about themselves. Bain was two years older and still a self-centered lover. She didn't want to compare them, but she knew that she had been missing out all these years. Being with a man as gorgeous as Gannon Wilcox would have any woman smiling day and night. He already had her smiling from a distance just looking at and admiring him. She let her eyes follow him to the back of the house where he jogged down toward the pier where she heard a noise. Moving to the back of the house, she wanted to see what was drawing him in that location.

Feeling like she should be ashamed for spying on him, she watched as he walked to the end of the pier where his family's boat was being pulled in. He must have had it driven down from where they kept it throughout the year when they weren't at the lake. She had never been on it before considering she had not been to the lake since that summer she broke up with him. Instead of returning to college for her senior year, she ran off and eloped with Blain, to her family's dismay. She hadn't been thinking then and was caught up in his fast talking and the fact that he was about to make it big. She saw stars and dollar signs wanted to live life in his fast lane, being admired by everyone. That lasted only a little while and most people, she later discovered, pitied her.

She watched Gannon talking to the guy who drove the boat and recognized him as someone from their childhood. The way Gannon laughed out loud and seemed happy, she wondered what impact his divorce had on his life, on his happiness. She didn't know the circumstances, but he didn't look like it was keeping him down. Hers, on the other hand, was still tearing her apart, which was her own fault. She should have broken all ties with Blain the minute she left him, but a glutton for punishment, she let his smooth, slick talking draw her back into his wild and crazy world.

She needed this time to figure out what was next for her. To her benefit, years ago, when she eloped with Blain to follow him, there wasn't a signing of any prenuptial agreement, making the settlement one she so richly deserved after years of being married to a slime. She now had money to do whatever she wanted with her life. All she had to do was figure out what her life was going to look like. For the next several months, she wanted to focus on finding herself again and would deal with her future further down the road.

Still watching them talk, she couldn't stop looking at everything about Gannon wondering if his hands still felt the same silky, smooth way on her skin. She wondered if his lips were still demanding and powerful, sending thrilled chills through her body. There was a time when all he had to do was say her name and she melted like butter right into his arms.

How could she walk away from a man who made her feel that way, for a man who never let her forget she was his trophy wife.

She was startled when her cell phone vibrated in her back pocket. Her sister was calling to face-time.

"Hey, Jenna!" she declared holding the phone up.

"Hey, baby sis. What are you up to and what happened to my visit? I thought you were coming to see us?"

Danielle had been meaning to tell Jenna she changed her mind about spending a few weeks with her family. She decided to follow her mother's advice and head right for the lake. If she had spoken to Jenna first, she would have allowed her to talk her into coming to Texas.

"I've been meaning to call you. I'm here at the lake. I'm sorry about the visit. I really needed this quiet time to sort some things out and I knew coming to your house, I would never get that done," she said.

"What are you trying to say? Are you saying my house is loud and out of order?" Jenna asked.

"Your words not mine," Danielle laughed.

"Yeah, I know how my house can be. One day when you have your own kids, you'll understand. Sometimes, it's better to let them run around and tire themselves out. I should take them to Benny's parents for a week and come spend a week at the lake with you."

Danielle tried to think of a reason to tell her no

without hurting her feelings. She suspected Jenna's husband, Benny, wouldn't be too keen on the idea either. If they were going to be kid free, he would want them to spend alone time together and not have Jenna away from him at the lake. Besides, she wanted to be alone, not entertaining her sister for a week.

"You wouldn't get past one day here without Benny showing up," she said and heard Jenna sigh on the other end.

"I know – you're right and my kids would call all day asking what I'm doing. I guess you could use this time alone after what you've been through. Can you believe that video of Blain and those two topless strippers is still making rounds on the internet? I'm sorry you had to go through all that. You had a crazy roller coaster ride with that class-less fool. What's next for you now that you have all that money and property?" Jenna asked.

Everyone asked her about that and she still didn't have much of an answer for that. One of the homes she planned to sell, but the house in Miami given to her in the divorce she planned on keeping. She loved the hot Miami weather.

"I don't know yet. Mom suggested I come to the lake and think about my next move. I'm thinking about going back to school and maybe even going to cosmetology school in order opening my own salon."

"You've always loved doing hair and you're good at it. You would run your own business! That would be hot. You should do it."

She had been thinking about it for a few years. When she mentioned it to Blain back when they were married, he told her to not waste her time because her job was to be his wife and be there when he needed her. Not once did she think more about her own dreams. She spent their time together helping him chase his. That was a mistake she'd never be able to do over.

Looking out of the window again, she looked at another mistake she made years ago, realizing she walked away from her happiness and wished she could go back and change things. She may be rich now, but after being married to Blain for so many years, money wasn't everything. It certainly didn't make her happy, though now, she smiled knowing she could stick it to Blain for how he treated her. She'd give it all away if she could go back in time and never give up on having a future with Gannon. She was young back then and leaving him was one of many wrongs she'd done and had no one to blame but herself. She turned back to the phone.

"I just may. How are the kids? Tell them I miss them! I may come visit at the end of the summer. By then, I intend to have a game plan in place for what's next for me."

"That sounds good. How's the house? Seen any fine men up there yet? The summer crowd is about to head that way which means a lot of fine men swimming on the lake."

Danielle laughed out loud.

"Leave it to you to have a one-track mind," she said.

"Hey, I'm married not dead!" Jenna proclaimed.

"Well, I haven't seen hardly anyone. I've only been here a few days and I'm been settling in, not really venturing out yet."

She looked toward Gannon. There was one hunk she forgot to mention.

"Have you a little fun with a lot of guys while you're there. You're single again and I need to live vicariously through you now that I'm an old married woman."

"Sis, stop it! You're far from old at thirty-two and I've never been one to have any kind of fun with a lot of guys. I'm a one-man kind of woman and you know that."

"Is it true that you've only been with two guys in your life? Gannon and Blain?"

Danielle gave her sister a stare that told her she'd crossed a line.

"How do you know how many men I've been with?" she asked pulling the phone away to grimace at it to be sure Jenna could see the look on her face.

"Girl, I know everything about you. You told me Gannon got your cookies on your eighteenth birthday and unless you were wild and slinging it when it went away to college, you went from Gannon to Blain. Am I wrong?" Jenna asked.

Danielle patted her feet in annoyance. She hated that her sister knew her so well.

"You're right, but that doesn't mean I want to be out slinging anything now. Speaking of Gannon, guess who's next door?" she asked.

"Gannon! Is he really? Is he by himself? With his family? With a woman? Is he still fine? I saw him at the services for his father and I swear every woman was foaming at the mouth at him. That brother is fine. I still can't believe you left him for Blain. I mean, Blain isn't hard on the eyes, but Gannon is like a walking god," Jenna screamed.

Danielle didn't need anyone reminding her of the error of her ways.

"He's here alone and you know he's divorced. Momma told me he filed for divorce from his wife and it's been final a little longer than mine."

"Right, I heard about that. Do you know what happened? I've been dying to know what woman would walk away from him, but then again, you did and I know you were insane!" Jenna laughed.

"Thanks for the support," she quipped.

"You know I'm just playing with you. Does he know you're there?"

"Yes. He came over a few days ago thinking mom and dad may be here to thank them for keeping the back of the property landscaped. He wasn't expecting to see me, but I'm glad he did. He's still as handsome and sexy as ever. I haven't had a good night's sleep since that day. I can't stop thinking about him and the mistake I made choosing Blain over him. I was so young and stupid back then," she said somberly.

"You were young, impulsive and very stupid back then, but you're beyond that now. You're single, he's single and you're both at the lake at the same time. Memories should be flying between the two of you like crazy. Feel free to jump his bones at your leisure. You have my permission," Jenna joked.

"I'm going to act like my sister didn't just tell me to mount a man who, deep down, probably still hates me. With that, I'm going to turn my phone off and go outside for some fresh air."

She laughed when Jenna rolled her eyes at her.

"Alright. I'm glad you're getting this time to yourself and on a serious note, this may be your time for a second chance with Gannon. If that ends up as an option, take it. He's a good man and you've had enough of snakes."

"I hear you. Love you, sis. I'll call you in a few days."

Putting her phone back in her pocket, she turned back to the window and focused on the fact that she and Gannon were at the lake at the same time. This was the place where their love once blossomed.

6

"She runs like a champ, Gannon."

"Thanks for bringing her down, Mike."

Gannon was thankful for the years of friendship with Mike, whom he met as a young boy on the lake. Now, he and his father ran a successful boating business.

"I had her checked out and washed from top to bottom. I know this was your father's pride and joy and I wanted to be sure we gave her some extra care until one of you requested that we bring her up to the lake. There are fresh linens and utensils and my pops did some paint touchups on the inside. The Anna-Marie is running like new."

Without going on board, Gannon gave the boat a once-over and liked what he saw. The metal parts were shining like a new penny and everything else looked like brand new white paint after a deep cleaning.

"Everything looks good, Mike. Thank you to you and your father for keeping the Anna-Marie in tip-top shape. She looks incredible! How's your family doing?" Gannon asked.

"Everyone is great. The lake area is our home now all year. After my father retired, he and my mom moved up here full-time and a few years ago after I got married, my wife fell in love with the area. She's an author and we realized she could do that from anywhere. My dad needed help running the business, so it was a perfect choice to move up this way permanently. I have a house on the other side of the lake. It's not as big as the properties on this side, but it's nice. I'm hoping to expand it soon. The Wilcox house is still the best looking one around here."

"Thanks for that. I have two of your wife's books. I love her espionage novels. I wish I had brought them up here with me so that I could get them autographed. I'm waiting on the next in the latest series!" Gannon declared.

"I'll let her know you enjoyed them. Anytime you want her to autograph your copies, let me know. We also have copies at the house and she can sign those for you anytime you want."

"I'll remember that."

"How is your mom doing?" Mike asked.

"She's coming along pretty good. It was rough once my dad first passed away, but my sisters and I have been sticking close to her, making sure she's good. My oldest sister, Kris, has been trying to get my mother to move in with her and her family, but you know my mom – she's her own woman and she loves living on her own. We each visit her often to keep her from drowning in sadness. Thankfully, my dad prepared her for life without him as soon as he found out he was sick."

"Is your family coming up this summer?" Mike asked.

"No. I'm here alone for the duration. I may be able to talk my mom into next year."

"Did I see Danielle the other day? I was at the market picking up some things for my wife and I thought I saw her at the check-out counter. I wasn't able to catch her before she left, but I was sure it was her."

Gannon looked up at her house and then back to Mike.

"It was probably her. She's here at her family's house for the summer. I talked with her briefly a few days ago."

Gannon saw a million questions and emotions on Mike's face. They were both thinking about a time when nothing and no one could keep the two of them apart.

"So, that was her. She was as pretty as ever. The two of you were glued at the hip for years. I heard she's now divorced from that music guy she was married to," Mike said.

"We were close at one point and then we grew up and grew apart. That's the way life goes, I guess."

Gannon noticed Mike looking at him as if he was

trying to get more from him by way of what happened. He had no plans of sharing.

"Right, right. Did you ever get married? Any kids?"

"I did get married, briefly, but we didn't have any children. We're now divorced."

"Sorry to hear that. You and Danielle made the perfect couple. Everyone assumed you would eventually get married, have some kids and spend your summers on the lake as a family. No two people were more perfect for each other than you and Danielle. It's a shame that things didn't work out. It seems as though you both picked the wrong spouses, no disrespect here," Mike explained.

"None taken and you're right as far as me. I can't answer for Danielle," he said.

"Well, perhaps we can ask her. She's headed this way," Mike said pointing.

Gannon turned around to see Danielle walking toward them. He watched her walk as her long black hair blew around in the mild wind that had begun to blow off of the water. He took note of the short denim jeans she wore and the white top that she tied around her slim waste. He loved her perfectly hour-glass shape, accentuated by her extra blossoming bosom, breasts he remembered making love to with his mouth in a way that would have her screaming his name. His body jumped as he moved around to adjust a part of him that twitched in desire at the sight of her. He couldn't believe his immediate reaction to her considering their past. It was that past that had him lusting after her. He was no longer bitter over their break-up, which was water under the bridge. He was seeing her with brand new eyes and he loved what he saw.

"Hey guys!" Danielle said approaching them. After watching them from the window, she felt like a stalker and decided to come out and say hello. There was no need for her to hide in her own house. The lake was as much hers as it was theirs. She remembered Mike from their childhood.

"Hi, Danielle!" Mike said giving her a hug. "I was just telling Gannon I thought I saw you earlier in the week at the store."

"You may have. I was there picking up a few things for the house. It's good to see you," she said and then turned to Gannon.

"Hi, Gannon."

Danielle felt odd the way her voice softened when she spoke to him. Everything in her felt mushy, soft and tender and it was because she was standing in front of Gannon, the man who had been starring in her dreams for the past two nights. When she woke in the morning, she ran to the bathroom to grab a much-needed cold shower.

"Hi, Danielle. You're looking as beautiful as the bright sunshine," he said.

"Thank you. I see you have the boat out. She is beautiful. My mom would talk about this boat like it belonged to her."

"You parents went out on her with my parents a lot during the summers they were here. How are you settling in at the house?" Gannon asked.

"Great. I'm finally all unpacked and my father had the house cleaned last week after I decided to come up, so there wasn't much to do other than enjoy it. I didn't realize how much I missed this place being gone from it for so long."

"Our parents have these houses for us to enjoy and you should have been doing that over the years."

Danielle, looked down and back up. She avoided the lake for years preferring following Blain around in hopes her presence would keep him from cheating on her. That didn't work.

"I know that now. I was too self-absorbed to realize that before."

"Mike, does your family still have their house on the other side of the lake?" she asked.

Danielle had to turn her attention away from Gannon. All she could think about when she saw him was her sister's advice to jump him. The image of them together had her feeling the need for another cold shower. Her body was on fire and she'd only been standing in front of him for a few seconds. Mike was a wonderful distraction.

"My parents live in it full-time, year-round now. I have a small house not right on the lake, but on the smaller bay side."

"You live here year-round, too?" she asked.

"I do and I love it. It's good seeing you back around these parts."

They all turned when a car horn honked from the street.

"Who's that?" Gannon asked not recognizing the car.

"That would be my wife coming to pick me up. I told her I was bringing your boat up and asked her to come around the lake and pick me up," Mike said.

"I would have been happy to take you back home after you brought the boat up today. I appreciate you making it a priority," Gannon said.

"It's not a problem. I'm glad you're here. I hope we can get together before the summer is over," Mike said.

"Let's do that. Next weekend, I'm planning on inviting some friends up for the day to swim, fish and hangout. I'm going to give the grill a workout and have some fun. Bring the wife and come on over," Gannon said.

The grin on Mike's face said it all. When they were kids, they hung out some, but not as much as Gannon hung out with his main crew and Danielle. There were times he was sure Mike felt like an outsider because his family lived on the other side of the lake. There was no separation as far as he was concerned and to him, they were friends and always would be.

"We're there and thanks for the invite. I better

hightail it before she honks again. We're picking the kids up from school. Danielle, it was good to see you."

"Same here," she said.

Gannon and Danielle watched Mike walk away and when silence became awkward, they smiled at each other.

"It shouldn't be this awkward, should it?" he asked.

Danielle exhaled.

"No, it shouldn't, but it is, isn't it?" she asked. Even though the moment was odd, she couldn't take her eyes off of his handsome face.

"I don't want it to be," he said softly, keeping his eyes focused directly on hers.

His baritone voice with its erotic undertone, sent a slight shiver through her body, a feeling she hadn't experienced in a long time. She used to love spending hours listening to him talk as the most salacious and amatory thought coursed through her. That was something that appears to have not changed.

"Neither do I, so let's not let it be."

"I agree," Gannon said and relaxed his stance, he knew turned rigid the moment she walked over. It wasn't because he didn't want to be in her presence, but it was due to the fact that he didn't want her to see how much he still desired her. Any old, bad feelings about their breakup were gone and were now replaced with a new zest for her.

"Are you taking the boat out on the open water soon?" she asked, breaking the intense moment.

"I might, not sure yet, but I will take her out for some fishing further down the lake and some days I'll just sit on her and enjoy the view. Since we're both here, maybe one day, you'd like to join me," he said.

Gannon didn't know where he was going with the invite, but hoped he hadn't crossed a line, making her feel uncomfortable. He didn't want his invite to sound like they were picking up on what they had years ago. He still considered her a friend.

"I would love that and she is a beauty."

"Great, we'll make a plan for that. What are you about to do?" he asked, not ready to leave her company yet.

"Nothing, really. I was going to grab a book and do some reading out on the deck."

"Have you had lunch yet? I was planning on throwing a few things on the grill and would love for you to join me if you didn't have any plans that I would take you away from."

Danielle could feel her pulse quicken. She would like nothing more than to share an afternoon lunch with him.

"I haven't eaten and grilled food sounds good. That was always my favorite here at the lake. There nothing like the taste of a grilled hot dog, burger or steak on the grill. I picked up a few things myself and was planning to throw some chicken breasts on the grill along with a salad I made. I can bring them with me," she offered.

"That's sounds good. I'm glad to see you still have that appetite, though it still doesn't show. Tell me if I'm complimenting you too much," he joked.

Danielle couldn't help how sexy he made her feel. She still loved hearing it, but no one made her feel the way he did when he complimented her.

"Keep them coming," she joked back and laughed.

"I've got a few hot dogs and some burgers and all the fixings. Come on, I'll walk you back up to get the salad and chicken and I'll get the grill started. I think this will help alleviate any awkwardness between us. The past is the past and I've let it go. How about you?" he asked.

"So have I," she smiled. When Gannon gave her his elbow, she looped her own arm in it and they walked back to their houses.

Danielle said a quiet thanks to the power of the lake. No one could have predicted she'd be walking alongside Gannon once again.

7

While Gannon cleaned off the grill, Danielle cleaned up the table of the discarded plates and extra food left over.

"You'll have enough for dinner or lunch tomorrow," she said while taking the containers inside.

"Feel free to take some with you. There is plenty for us both to split. That marinated chicken breast was delicious. What did you put on it?" he asked.

"A combination of seasonings with the main one's being herb and garlic. I used a recipe my mother gave me. I put them in the container this morning to cook later, giving the flavor time to marinate throughout each piece."

"Well, you certainly put your foot in that," Gannon declared.

"You cooked them just right."

Finishing with the grill, Gannon closed the top and put the last bit of trash in the can.

"I'm glad you enjoyed it. I never grill when I'm home and I don't know why. I have a deck out back with an industrial size grill that is still as clean as the day I bought it," he laughed.

"I'm sure you've been focusing on work and that's understandable."

"Listen, I'm going to grab a beer. Would you like one or a glass of wine? It's a beautiful day and the sun will be setting in a few hours, a sight I'm looking forward to seeing. I love the way the moon cascades off the lake as it's rising. You can join me if you like," he said.

"I'd love to and a glass of wine would be great."

"Red or white?" Gannon asked, happy he was going to have a little more time with her.

"White."

"Coming right up. Have a seat and I'll get it."

Entering the house, he looked back at her and at the same time, she looked at him and their eyes locked with neither saying a word. He could clearly see the pulse in her neck strumming hard as if her heart beat was speeding up. In the past, that meant that she was thinking of making love with him as they would often sneak away to do. There was a pull between them that even time couldn't make fade away. Breaking the stare, he turned toward the kitchen.

Danielle sat down on one of the four recliners on the deck with a perfectly clear view of the lake. She smiled at the way the universe works. Who would have thought that she would be spending a few hours with Gannon Wilcox after the past they shared? In case it never happened again, she was going to enjoy the moment.

"Here you go," Gannon said handing her a glass and joining her by straddling the recliner right next to her.

"The lake is an amazing place. It's like, you can shut the entire world out and focus on the beauty and solitude of this magnificent view. I have missed being up here. I've been gone for far too long."

"Life happened and you went with it," he said.

"I did and looking back, I should not have. I never should have let anything or anyone keep me from my family. I spent more time running around behind Blain than finding my own way."

"Were you ever happy in your marriage?"

Gannon heard himself ask the question, but didn't look at her. They were sharing and it was probably time that they did.

"No, not one day and I know that now."

"Tell me," he said. He knew he should explain more, but that was all he was able to get out without making reference to the fact that they never had closure on that part of their life back then.

"All of it?" she asked.

"Yes."

"I'm sorry," she said.

"Don't." He did turn to her after her apology. "Don't ever apologize for making a decision for your own life, good or bad. Whatever the outcome, it was your decision and you did what you thought was best for you whether it was or not. We were young and had high expectations for a future neither of us had a clue of what that actually meant."

"Thank you for that, but I owed you an explanation and I never did that. I was wrong. You really want to know about my life?" she asked.

"Yes. I have all night. I'm listening."

Danielle took a sip of her wine and leaned back.

"It was awful pretty much from the start. I can admit I never slept with him while you and I were together. In fact, it didn't happen until I was married to him. I never broke your trust in that way with anyone while I was at school or any other time. I just got caught up in Blain's stardom."

"I never saw you as the type of woman to sleep around, so I never doubted that."

Danielle smiled. That was one hurdle. Until she married Blain, Gannon had still been her one and only.

"The night we got married, we eloped to Vegas a few days after my twenty-first birthday. The night before the wedding should have been a sign that I was with the wrong man. We were eloping, so I hadn't told anyone, but he told all of his friends and they met us in Vegas. My family thought I was going back to school early. Blain had it all planned out and he received a large advance and I was stupidly blinded. I was there alone and he had his crew with him. He had just signed a major record deal and wanted me with him. I refused to go as some kind of groupie, so one day he said he wanted to fly to Vegas and get married because he was moving to California and he wanted me with him. I later found out that his friends took him to some girlie club while I was in the hotel room alone. He didn't come back until right before the noon appointment at the chapel. Turns out, he spent the night with two women to celebrate. I had heard his friends talking about getting him the hookup for his last final night as a single man and I brushed it off. My entire marriage was like that, woman after woman, scandal after scandal until one day I could no longer take it. Our lives were smeared all over the tabloids and it got to the point that he would have a prepared response to every photo or video of him. His antics hurt me to my core. I finally got up the nerve to leave him and find Danielle again and believe me, I will never be a doormat for anyone!" she declared and took another sip.

"Good for you because you deserve better. You deserve a man who will be honest and true to you and who will allow you to be you. A marriage or even a relationship should never be one-sided. I hope you know you deserve better than that," Gannon said.

"You never would have treated me like that. That's not even a question because I already know it to be true. I know things didn't work out with your wife, but I have no doubt it wasn't because you cheated or treated her horribly."

"You're right it wasn't. I met her while on one of my tours, thought I had fallen head over heels in love with her, but it turns out, I fell in love with who I thought she was and not who she really was. You know I've always wanted children and I thought she did, too. Turns out, that was a lie we lived for a few years until I found out for years, she had been taking birth control and I didn't know it. I thought we were having problems conceiving and all along, she was hiding the fact that she didn't want children. She made up fake doctor appointments to get examined to find out why we weren't getting pregnant. The appointments I accompanied her to, she always wanted to go in without me and even sent me to a specialist to see if I was the problem. Turns out it was her desire to lead me on. Once I found out what she had done, I was furious. She then said she never wanted to have children and family is important to me. I filed for divorce and we went our separate ways. It was a lesson learned for me and like you, I realized I deserved better than that."

"I know this may sound odd, but have you ever thought about what our lives would be like if we had stayed together and I hadn't made the worst decision of my life?"

Danielle asked because she had thought about that very thing many times, even while she was married to Blain. She realized early that Gannon was the one she let get away.

"I have and I know for a fact we would have a few little ones running around by now," he joked.

"We both wanted kids. Looks like my ex-husband decided he wanted them too, but not with me. He's got several paternity tests pending and I found out he's been secretly paying child support for a little boy who's three years old. The problem is, every time I mentioned I was ready for a baby, he had another story of why we should wait."

Gannon shook his head in disgust. This is why women found men so untrustworthy.

"He's the worst kind of man, the kind that gives other men a bad reputation whether they are good or bad."

"Not you though. No one could ever tarnish the remarkable man you are."

"Thank you and you're quite wonderful yourself, I'm sure. The good part of all of this is that we knew when to walk away to find our own happiness. I believe there is greatness in store for us both."

"I agree. This wine is good."

"Remember the first time you drank wine and how drunk you got?" Gannon asked and they broke out into a fit of laughter.

"I remember being in the back of your father's car overlooking the cliff. I've never been that sick before in my life, but you took care of me by rubbing my back and using a bottle of water and a napkin to pat my head to cool me off."

"Wow, the cliff. I haven't thought about that spot in a long time."

Gannon now had vivid memories of the times they snuck off there to be alone. It was their spot.

"Really? That was our go-to place when we wanted to get away from everyone and be together."

Gannon thought about their perfect spot. It was a few miles down the hill off of the main road and they would drive their, take food with them and spend hours together.

"Those were some good days," he acknowledged.

"We had a lot of them. This lake has always held a special part of my heart, a part where you've always lived."

Danielle turned to look at Gannon when he turned around. Perhaps, she'd said too much or maybe it was the wine. She'd only had a few sips, so maybe not.

"You never forget your first love. You were mine," he said with a serious tone. He wanted her to know that she should never question how genuine their time together was.

"You were mine, too."

The moment continued in complete silence as their eyes met and connected.

Danielle looked at Gannon and saw all that she'd walked away from. He was a man who loved deeply and honestly and any woman lucky enough to be the recipient was the luckiest girl in the world. She sought fame instead of love and it got her years of embarrassment and a divorce. She had found love on the lake and walked away from it. A smarter woman would have known better, but she had been thinking like a girl, not a woman. Now, she was a woman and what she wanted most was the man sitting across from her. Gannon still held her heart.

Gannon let her words sink in and along with the look in her eyes, there was still love for him there. He understood because the moment she opened the door when he knocked, their past overwhelmed him and he remembered their love. Some would say it was his first love experience, but he knew it was the most important one and now, he still loved her.

"We've been sitting out here so long, the sun is going down," Gannon said.

"I guess we'll get to see the beautiful moonlit sky. I hope you don't mind the company," Danielle said and smiled over at him.

"I don't mind at all. I couldn't ask for better company."

Turning back to check out the beautiful night, Gannon knew he was in trouble. He was in love. Years ago, he had fallen in love on the lake and today, he was there again.

8

After a week at the lake house, Gannon was preparing for his first party of the summer. He was walking around his house getting things set up with an extra pep in his step. His happiness was due to the fact that he had about twenty friends coming up for the party along with Mike and his wife and most excitedly, he was happy that Danielle had decided to join them. She had even offered to make her mother's famous double chocolate cupcakes.

After that night on his deck, they had shared more time together. That next morning, he'd invited her out on the boat to go fishing and they spent the day out further down the lake where the fish were swimming and plentiful. Later, as they brought the boat back in, they donned bathing suits and he almost had a heart attack when Danielle removed her shorts and top and revealed a sexy, hot pink two-piece bathing suit that practically made him forget his own name. Seeing her in the flesh took him back to a time when his hands roamed her curves as he drove her wild. Now, she was filled out like a woman should be, lush in all the right places and toned where it counted. He was a lost cause and he knew it. He had to wait to take off his own shorts knowing his swim trunks would show how his body reacted to seeing all of her.

They had settled into a comfortable place with each other and each day, they found a reason to see each other. They even went shopping at the local market the day before to pick out things he needed for his party. He'd picked up tons of steaks, burgers, hotdogs, shrimp and lobsters as they shopped like a couple having an event together.

His sisters were coming up for the party and were bringing various salads and desserts with them. He'd hired a friend to act as bartender for the night and even had the pool guy make sure the pool was ready for use. He purchased extra chairs to sit around the pool and extra lighting to keep the back area of the house well-lit for the evening or until his last guest left or passed out in the house. Anyone unable to drive home would be invited to spend the night. There may not be enough beds, but there was enough space, including the recliner chairs on the deck.

He was looking forward to the party, not just to see his friends, but because he could spend another entire evening lusting after Danielle. They had been flirting with each other all week and he wanted to ask her out on an official date, but remained hesitant about what it would mean. There was no need in fighting the attraction that had developed between them again.

They were dancing around the fact that they wanted each other and he saw no reason to deny it any longer. They were two adults, no longer teenagers and nothing should prevent them from spending time together without worrying about crossing any invisible lines. Neither were married anymore. Why were they dancing around each other? Tonight, he would focus on the party and tomorrow, he would take the next step.

Gannon turned when he heard a knock on the front door. He must have a guest arriving very early. Rushing to it, he opened it to find his sisters standing with their hands full of containers of food.

"Why didn't either of you use a key?" he asked taking some of the food from them and turning around.

"Do you see all this food? There's more in the car, so go get it," Dawn said.

"Looks like you brought enough food to feed an army."

"We did and we invited about ten more people. I wanted to be sure we had enough food. Mom also sent crab cakes and you know how good her crab cakes are," Kris said.

"Crab cakes! Are you serious?" Gannon said excitedly.

"Dead serious and she said to tell you to have a good time. She's happy you're making the best of being here. I showed her the pictures you sent us of you on the boat. Who took the pictures of you?" Dawn asked as Gannon whizzed back and forth from the car to the house.

"Danielle," he said and kept moving as if saying her name was the most natural thing in the world.

Dawn and Kris looked at each other and then looked at how nonchalant he uttered Danielle's name.

"That's all we get? You say Danielle's name like it's not something that would stop us both in our tracks. Danielle is here on the lake and on the boat with you?"

Gannon placed the two bags in his arms on the table and headed back for the front door to get the last of the food and the extra lights he asked them to bring.

"Gannon, stop moving!" Dawn shouted at him.

He stopped just before going back out the door and waited for the barrage of questions. He figured it would be best to respond honestly since Danielle would be at the party.

"You said Danielle. Danielle Fenton is here or is there another Danielle you're talking about."

Gannon turned around and faced the firing squad.

"Yes, Danielle Fenton, used to be Danielle Combs is here on the lake at her parents' house. She's staying in it for the summer after her divorce and we were out on the boat the other day. You'll see her in a few. She's baking cupcakes for the party and should be over soon. She's coming to help set everything up."

Dawn and Kris looked between each other before

looking back at their brother, again. Both were stunned that he could say her name so easily.

"Are you crazy to say it like we would talk about the weather? You say it like it's something we should already know. You've been up here for a week and Danielle has been, too and you failed to say anything about that in the phone calls we've had with you? Are you playing with us right now?" Dawn asked, the most outspoken.

Gannon grinned, knowing he'd caught them off-guard.

"I'm not playing and yes she's here."

"So, it's some kind of coincidence that you're both here at the same time?" Dawn asked.

"Yes, Dawn, it is. We're both getting over our divorces and it just so happens that she knew the value of being on the lake when it comes to peace of mind just like I do. Don't read more into it than that."

"Things are good between you then?" Kris asked.

"That was years ago and we were young. The past is the past."

"Right, but does that mean there's a future?" Dawn asked.

Gannon knew the conversation wasn't ending any time soon. He could see the barrage of questions waiting to come out of both of his sisters.

"Let it go and start setting things up. You can grill me later. Guests will be arriving soon," Gannon said turning and heading back to the car.

"There might be hope for him yet," Dawn said.

"I'm already claiming we'll have a new sister-in-law before the end of the summer, the one we should have had all along. I'm going over to say hello to Danielle," Kris said.

"Not without me!" Dawn declared and left the house through the back, forgetting about helping Gannon with the food. They once considered Danielle a little sister. From the look of things, their brother was once again smitten. They were close and both knew the signs in his responses to them and his demeanor.

**

Danielle walked around her house like a madwoman, cooking, cleaning and dressing at the same time. She told Gannon she would make cupcakes and also decided to make banana pudding cups, a favorite dessert they shared as kids. She had also offered to help him set everything up and was already running behind.

She'd spent most of the morning trying to decide on the perfect outfit. All week, she and Gannon had spent practically every day together and she loved every minute of it. They talked more about their lives for the years when they'd lost contact and found that though they'd each had some struggles, overall, life had been good to them.

After he'd left the service, he'd gone to college and was a few credits away from his degree, something he was planning on remedying really soon. He was then planning on getting his graduate and doctorate degrees so that he could be the best chief executive officer of his company because the employees deserved his best. She had shared with him that she had dreams of finishing school with only the one year left that she never completed, focusing on business management. She then wanted to go to cosmetology school and open up her own spa that offered women more than just hair care, but body care as well. It turned out he was as excited as she was about the possibilities that were ahead of her. For the first time in a long time, she felt motivated to follow her own dreams.

After finding the perfect outfit, a white and blue flowing sundress and the perfect heels, she worked on packaging the food up to take next door when she heard a knock at the back door. Thinking it was Gannon coming to check on her, she rushed to open it and smiled brightly when she saw Kris and Dawn standing on the other side beaming brightly at her.

"Oh, my goodness!" she screamed after opening the door and gave both a sisterly hug.

"We didn't believe it when Gannon said you were here. Give me another hug!" Dawn said. Of the two sisters, she had been the closest to Danielle growing up.

During their times on the lake as young girls, they were older than her, but still they allowed her to hang with them and their friends. It had been years since they'd last set eyes on her.

"He mentioned both of you were coming for the party and I was excited. It's been too long since we've seen each other."

"I know and to think you're here at the same time as Gannon. How coincidental can that be?" Kris asked.

"Very. I was shocked when I opened the door and on the other side stood Gannon looking all hot and sexy as ever. Your brother has gotten even better looking with time, as if that were even possible. He was always the most handsome guy in the world. Come on in while I finish packing everything up. We have a lot to catch up on!" Danielle said cheerfully.

"Yes, we do, but first, we need to know if anything is going on between you and Gannon? If so, we're happier than you will ever know. If not, then what can we do to make it happen? You know you were always meant to be a Wilcox!" Dawn proclaimed.

Danielle knew one thing for sure and that was, she had never heard truer words.

"I know and I appreciate you saying that. Nothing has happened yet, but I don't doubt that something is going on. Neither of us has made a move, but this week has been fun. We went fishing and he took me out on the Anna-Marie. I went running with him one morning and we've shared several evenings enjoying being on the lake. Last night, we walked down to the pier and sat there throwing rocks out on the water like we did as kids. This lake is magical. It's a place that is made for love," she said.

"Love? You're still in love with Gannon?" Kris asked.

Without any hesitation, Danielle was ready to boldly proclaim her feelings.

"Yes, I am. I don't know if he will ever be able to love me back again, but I do love him and this week showed me I always have. Maybe I wasn't mature or ready for the love I feel for him now, but if there is any chance that I could get a second chance with him, I want it. I gave up a wonderful thing for the high-life and that was a mistake. Fate had a hand in us being here at the same time and it's supposed to mean something. We're back on the lake where we first fell in love and we're both here alone. We'll have nothing, but time and if that time connects us again, I'm ready for it."

"Yeah!" Dawn cheered. "When he was telling us that you were here, we could hear something different in his voice. He's still hooked on you, too and that's a good thing. Let us help you get this food over to the house and we're keeping our fingers crossed that something works out between you two. How long are you staying on the lake? All summer?"

"I'll be here all summer," Danielle slurred with delight.

"Yes, girl! Get it!" Dawn exclaimed and they all

chuckled.

"Gannon probably will be, too, now that you're here. I know he'll be taking some trips back to the company, but for the most part, the company is running itself and he needed the time off. He's been going to school and running the company since my dad first got sick and he needs this break. I'm trying to convince him to stay the whole summer and come to town when he needs to. He trusts Kris and I enough to let us run things in his absence and it's going well."

"He's been pretty relaxed since he arrived and he's been doing a lot of fun things and not a lot of work."

"That's good to know. Now, we need him to focus on his personal life and all will be well," Kris said.

"Let's get to the house. I need to get these banana pudding cups in the refrigerator," Danielle said.

As she followed Dawn and Kris next door, Danielle felt better than she had in years. She wasn't sure if his family held any ill-will toward her after how she treated Gannon, but she was glad to know they were forgiving enough to see that everyone makes mistakes and are willing to move on. Secretly, she hoped she could move on with Gannon.

9

"Did you have a good time?" Gannon asked as he and Danielle walked arm in arm to her house following his party. It was two in the morning and the party had finally wound down. For those who were staying the night, he made sure everyone had a place to sleep inside. There were sleeping bags and blankets all over the house. They had blown up two air mattresses and as far as he knew, no one complained about an awkward sleeping arrangement.

After cleaning up after the party, covering the pool and putting the protective locks in place, everyone retreated indoors where a smaller party continued. Once everyone was settled, it was time to make sure Danielle got home safe, even though her house was a stone's throw away.

"I had a wonderful time."

"In case I didn't mention this before, you look incredible tonight," Gannon said the minute they reached the back-sliding glass door. When she turned to face him, he couldn't fight his desire for her that had been building all week, finally coming to a peak at the party. He watched as she interacted with everyone and her interactions were as comfortable as if they were a couple, hosting the party together. His friends loved and adored her and a few even wondered if he was planning on being more than just a next-door neighbor. Internally, he was hoping for the same.

Danielle was resigned to the fact that the time had come for them to stop acting as if they weren't hot for each other. She was also thinking of much more than the physical attraction, but for now, looking at him standing in front of her all virile and sexy, she couldn't think of anything else but lips she wanted to kiss and arms she wanted to be in more than she wanted her next breath. She looked at him and wished he could read her mind or at least sense her desire for him. She wouldn't survive if he did want her as much as she wanted him.

"Thank you. It took me most of the morning to find the perfect dress. Can I be honest and tell you I chose this one hoping you would like it?"

Here goes nothing, she thought. It was sink or swim time.

"Really? You thought about me when you were wondering what to wear? I like knowing that and you hit it out the park with this," he said reaching up and running his finger along the strap that covered her shoulder. "You are so beautiful," he added and kept his eyes locked on hers.

"You make me feel beautiful when you look at me. I

love how it feels to be around you again."

"I love being around you. I don't want you to think that I'm ignoring the fact that we're attracted to each other, which is also obvious to everyone else around us. I'm wondering if I should follow my heart right now," he said.

"What is your heart telling you?" she asked.

"It's telling me to kiss you because I've been dying to do so all week."

Danielle was barely keeping it together. If Gannon didn't soon kiss her, she would have to take the lead and kiss him. Her desire for him was immeasurably off of any scale. It wasn't just her body that wanted and needed him, it was her entire being. He is what she missed and needed. She missed having a man look at her the way he was looking at her as if nothing else in the world mattered but her.

"Are you going to do what your heart is telling you to do?"

She hoped beyond hope that his answer would be yes.

Gannon didn't want to answer with words. Instead he leaned down from his six-foot five height, to her five-foot seven level and before either of them could say another word, he kissed her and not just with a simple kiss. The scorching coming together of their lips packed a wallop that had her yearning, wanting more, much more.

If the world was spinning around them, Gannon

didn't know it because he was caught up in a vortex of nothingness, except for feeling, want and need. His body hummed to life as his lips caressed hers and with the powerful way she was returning his kiss, he'd made the right decision.

Gannon took his time kissing her first right on the lips and then taking his time kissing across the seam of her lips from one end to the other making sure to taste every part of her that he could. A fierce strike of light gleamed across his mind as his world turned sideways the moment he felt her tongue snake out to meet his before he melded their mouths together. He then moved his mouth to the side of her face, kissing her cheek and when she moaned, he moved further to her ear, taking the lobe between his lips to suck on it before kissing around it lightly, just enough to elicit more erotic moans from her. Danielle didn't disappoint with her reaction to him.

"This is leading to something," he whispered in her ear as he felt her body tremble against him.

Danielle moved her head backward to look up at him.

"I hope so," she replied softly on a hush. She was too turned on to say much more.

Gannon's mind and body were on fire like never before. He hadn't felt an intense pull of want and craving in many years, not since the last time he had kissed her. The feelings were still there. When he briefly pulled back, his eyes traveled to Danielle's lips at the exact moment she stuck her tongue out again and licked her lips where his has just been. Growling with need, he didn't wait to pull her into his arms and kissed her again, this time deepening the kiss, pouring into it every bit of lust-filled desire he could muster up. As appealing as it was to be standing with Danielle in his arms, he didn't want to do so standing out on her deck. He needed to take things indoors.

"Are you going to invite me in?' he said when he could breathe again. He wasn't the only one having an amorous response to their kiss. He could see Danielle was trying to get her body back in check.

"No invitation needed. Just come in," she said and turned to unlock the door.

Taking Gannon by the hand, she pulled him inside and locked the door. Before they could move even an inch, he reached down and picked her up, encircling his hips with her legs as he pressed her securely against the glass door and devoured her mouth. They went at each other as if this kiss was going to be their last kiss, ever. It was desperate, efficient and tantalizing, causing them both to moan loudly showing their appreciation that they were finally in each other's arms.

Danielle wasn't sure she was still living and breathing. The kiss had caused her to travel to another dimension unlike anything she'd ever experienced before. With her legs snug around his waist, she delighted in the feel of his hands all over her body. She caressed his shoulders and his neck until her hands reached his head as she pressed him even closer. The moment she opened her mouth, her body sizzled with a deep, burning passionate fire that only he could put out.

"I want you," she boldly said.

"I know you can feel how much I want you. I'm right here for the taking, baby," he responded. "We need a soft place," he uttered between kisses.

"Sofa, behind you," she said as he moved into action, turning them around and walking with her in his arms to the nearest soft spot.

Coming up against it, he placed her down and followed her, finding a comfortable spot between her outstretched legs. He looked at her, taking in her beauty, thankful that he was once again with the woman he seemed to have always held his heart.

"This isn't crazy right? We're not losing our minds with lust, are we?" he asked.

Danielle smiled.

"I sure hope so. I meant it when I said I want you. I have all week and right now, I'm happier and more delighted than I've been in a long time. I'm in your arms, where I was always meant to be. I hope that doesn't sound corny because it's true."

"Danielle, there is nothing corny about how you feel because it mirrors what I'm feeling, too and you're right, in my arms is where you were always meant to be. We're here. You and me. We're here and I don't want to waste any more time."

"Love me," Danielle uttered on a sigh.

Before she could say another word, Gannon's lips covered hers as his hands reached for the hem of her dress, pulling it up and over her head, tossing it to the floor beside them. As his gaze followed the length of her body, she felt a delightful zing flow through her watching the way he admired her.

"Time has changed us both and you are sexier than any woman I've ever laid eyes on. You are even more beautiful than I remember and I still remember everything about you." He kissed her lips while he talked. "I remember how soft your skin always felt and still does. I remember never getting enough of kissing you, just like now. Most of all, I remember how our bodies were always in sync like we were created to make love only to each other. Some things you never forget and being with you is one of those things."

Danielle's entire body was screaming yes as they continued kissing passionately.

Blood rushed through Gannon's body as he took in his fill of her. As she lay beneath him, he was thankful for the moon that shone through the windows, casting a glow on them and letting him see her in all of her glory. He looked her up and down taking in the thin straps of the black lace thong that circled her hips. He let his eyes wonder up to the black strapless bra that blocked her breasts from his view. Reaching between them, he unsnapped the front closure and watched as the cups that covered her large, full breasts broke away and before him, the mounds pebbled under his view. Leaning down, he tasted one peak and then the other and loved that she squirmed in delight under him. They moaned together, heightening the intensity of the moment.

"You have on too many clothes," Danielle said, reaching for his shirt and tugged it until she was able to pull it up and over his head. Before she reached for anything else, she ran her hands over his muscled chest.

"Your hands feel hot against my skin," he said. "I love how you feel," he added.

"You are not that young boy I was in love with so many years ago. You feel amazing and all man," she said and reached for the belt of his jeans.

Knowing they weren't going to be able to get his jeans off while laying on top of her, Gannon stood and removed them while reaching in his wallet and pulling out one of the two condoms he kept there. He wasn't one to sleep from woman to woman, but he never wanted to be caught in a situation where he needed one and didn't have it. He would rather have one and not need it. For Danielle, he had a feeling he would need them both.

Placing the condom between his teeth, he reached down and removed his boxer briefs before rejoining her on the sofa where he reached for her thong and slid the barely-there material down her toned, model-like legs. With both of them naked, he didn't want to waste too much time indulging in the act of making love to her.

"Now that you have me here, naked, what do you plan to do with me?" Danielle purred.

"Oh, baby, you have no idea. That's a powerful question and believe me, I intend to show you and not just tell you. I hope you're ready for me?"

Danielle couldn't speak as the force of the power surrounding them enveloped her, causing her to internally beg for him to get inside of her.

Placing the condom over his hardened member, Gannon rejoined her on the sofa, planting himself between her already wide spread legs.

Leaning down, he took her lips in a commanding kiss while reaching between them to prepare her body for his entry. Finding her already wet and ready for him, there was no preparation needed. She was where he was.

Kissing down her body, he found her breasts and after kissing around the large globes, he took the nub of one into his mouth and kissed and licked it until it was as hard as a pebbled rock.

"Yes!" Danielle moaned. "That feels so good," she added and held on to his head as it wound around and around from one side of her body to the other, causing her temperature to rise. As his head moved, her hips began a slight grind of their own as she felt his penis long and thick between her legs, almost as if it were searching for her sweet spot. She was ready to feel him inside.

"You ready for me, darlin'?"

"More than ready. I need you," she begged.

Gannon reached for her legs, pulling her knees up higher and finding a comfortable place between them. Using one hand, he guided himself into her body, slowly. He wanted to take his time and enjoy the snug feeling of being inside of her body again, but he couldn't. Danielle pushed up, causing him to slide deeper into her body and he was lost. He pushed all the way in and on an exhale, he withdrew only to surge back in again.

Taking her mouth, he kissed her and moved his tongue around inside of her mouth the same way his body was moving in and out of hers. As Danielle held on tightly to his shoulders and wrapped her legs around his waist, he gave her all that he had. They rode each other delighting in the sound of a moan here, a gasp there and a grunt laced in between. The chair moved with his powerful strokes and the way Danielle met him stroke for stroke and whispered in between kisses how good he was making her feel, he knew he wouldn't be able to last long and he wanted her with him.

Adding a swirl to his hips, he gave her all of him with long, determined strokes just as he felt her body gave in to the demand for release.

Danielle was flying higher than she ever

remembered being before. Leaning her head into the space between Gannon's head and shoulder, she screamed out her release as it slammed into her over and over again. Her hips continued their powerful response to his plunges in and out of her body as if they had a mind of their own. She was floating and then flying as she gripped him with her arms around his neck while the muscles in the lower part of her body gripped him. Rockets exploded behind her eyes as white lights flashed across her lids. She continued to delight in how exquisitely Gannon rode her through her orgasm. Wanting him to experience the same, she gripped his member tightly with each pass into her body knowing the sensation would send him over the edge into a sexually enhanced bliss where she was.

Gannon's head was about to explode as his body burned like fire. Hearing Danielle's soft mewls and whimpers and the feel of her soft body gripping him, he let go and rode out an orgasm that threatened to take his very breath away.

He groaned out his pleasure as he fiercely pumped uncontrollable yet determined thrusts, calling her name over and over as wave after wave of pleasure consumed him. His body moved on its own accord until he was able to gather enough control to slow his body down as his body attempted to calm. Never before had he experienced anything as powerful as what his body had just endured.

Pulling back, he looked down at Danielle to be sure

she was okay and found her trying to breathe easy again as he was trying to do.

"Hello sweetness," he said once he could speak again.

"Hello yourself."

"My appetite for you was ravenous like I've never experienced before. I've been waiting all week to make love to you like this," he declared softly as he placed soft kisses on her lips. Releasing her legs, he caressed them as he moved so that they were next to each other, taking his weight off of her.

"I've been waiting all week for you to make love to me and I must say it was well worth the wait," Danielle admitted.

Gannon pulled her closer, placing his head on her chest, kissing her breasts since his head rested there.

"I guess the awkwardness of that first day is gone," he joked, causing them both to chortle.

"I would say so and I'm glad. I don't want to be awkward around you. I want to be right where I am now," Danielle said.

"As much as I love being with you on this sofa, it limits our movements. If we can get to a bed, I want to hold you in my arms all night."

"What about your house guests?" she asked.

"They can fend for themselves. The doors are locked and I'm sure they're all sleep or passed out by now. As for you and me, my focus is on us and when daylight comes, I want to be with you."

Danielle kissed him. "I want that, too."

"Bed?" he asked.

"Yes, a bed and bring the other condom. I'm sure we're going to need it."

Gannon stood and picked Danielle up in his arms, tossing her over his shoulder as she giggled out loud. Reaching for his wallet, he withdrew the other condom and took the steps two at a time. Nothing else mattered except them and making love to her again.

10

Gannon woke as the sun beamed on his face. As the day came into focus, he felt in front of him and delighted in the thought that he had not dreamt making love to Danielle all night. Exhausted from their amorous activities, he had a feeling the sun had been up for a while, but once slumber had finally come to them, they were down for the count from pure exhaustion. Still, he was awake and so was his body the moment he felt Danielle's luscious backside press back against the front of him.

He caressed her body under the blanket that now covered them. He wasn't sure how that had happened because once they reached the bed, their lovemaking had turned so wild, the blankets that covered the bed had ended up on the floor. The last thing he remembered was sleep overtaking his body after they made love as if they were doing it for the last time.

Leaning forward, he kissed Danielle's exposed shoulder while his hands roamed her body under the blanket.

"If you're not careful, I'll never let you out of this

bed," she whispered on a yarn causing him to laugh.

"I'm sorry. I had to make sure you were real and not a mirage. I was questioning whether I was dreaming about you or if you were really in my arms."

Danielle moved around until his body hardened for her again.

"You feel pretty real to me," she said, giggling.

"In a minute, things are about to get even more real if you don't stop moving around like that. Making love to you in the light of day would be a dream except for the fact that we don't have any more condoms. We used up all the ones I had with me."

Danielle turned around in his arms.

"You know, you taught me a lot about pleasing you years ago and it wasn't always about you being inside of me. There are other things we can do and the way my body is on fire again for you, I'd be disappointed if we didn't indulge."

Without waiting for his response, she moved so that Gannon was lying flat on his back under her.

"I like the way you think," he said.

With no more words needed, Danielle slid down his body, kissing a path as she went. She didn't know if what they were sharing would happen again and just in case it didn't, she wanted to share as much with him as she could. Memories of how he taught her to pleasure him filled her head as her head moved down his body and she came eye level with that part of him that made her body come alive for him. She couldn't wait to show him how much she loved having him in her arms and in her bed again.

**

Gannon walked into his lake house not sure of what the scene would look like. He assumed he would find a house full of people left from the night before sleeping in every spare space available. Surprisingly, the house was empty, furniture was back in order and the extra linens that everyone used were already in bags ready for the laundry. He would call a service to pick them up later.

He should have known everyone would be gone. When he finally left Danielle's bed, he checked the time and it was already close to noon, much later than he thought. It was clear that not even his sisters were worried about his whereabouts. As he went through the house, neither of them was still there, really surprising him. He thought they would hang around to ask him about his disappearing act in the middle of the night. On the refrigerator, he found a note in Dawn's handwriting.

We hope you had a good night. The party was great and tell Danielle we said good for her. Don't let her get away a second time. You were always meant for each other. We cleaned up, so go back to Danielle's and have fun. Call us later. Love you, bro.

Both of his sisters had signed the note. He was elated knowing that they supported him knowing he had left to walk Danielle next door the night before and they assumed correctly that he had been with her all-night. Even now, Danielle was sound asleep in her bed after a night of exhausting yet pleasurable lovemaking. He didn't know what was next for them, but his sisters were right that he and Danielle were a perfect fit as they had been years ago. He had no plans of letting her go a second time. They had reconnected and he looked forward to building something with her if she was willing.

He was about to take a quick shower to try and get a run in even though the heat had already risen for the day when his cell phone rang before he made it halfway up the stairs. It was his mother.

"Hey, mom. Is everything alright?" he asked.

"Of course, Gannon. Everything is fine. I was calling to see how your party went and if you enjoyed the crab cakes," she said.

"The party was great and the cupcakes were a hit as usual."

"I'm glad to hear it. Are you enjoying your time at the lake house? I know you needed this time to slow down and do something other than work and hopefully you are doing that," she said.

"I am and it's been good. I may stay a few extra weeks, coming into the office for a day or two, but driving back to North Carolina to stay at the lake. I love it here. Speaking of the lake, I got the most interesting phone call last night."

"Is that so?" Gannon already knew she was going to

say she had talked to Danielle's mother and found out that Danielle was also at the lake.

"Yes. Millie called me last night to check in and said that Danielle was at their lake house. Have you seen her yet?"

Gannon smiled. His mother was never sly enough to hide her intentions. He knew her too well.

"Yes, I have seen and talked to her."

"How is she? Did you remember I told you she was divorced?"

"Mom, the world knows she's divorced. Their rocky marriage and divorce was headline news for months."

"Yes, she was married to some star who sang music or something. Anyway, how is she? Is she still single?"

"Didn't Danielle's mother give you the full run-down on her life? I'm sure she did," he chuckled. He loved how his mother attempted to play cool.

"She did, but I was wondering what was going on between the two of you now that you're both single."

"Ma, if anything was going on, I wouldn't share that with you. You're my mother. I will tell you that we have been spending some time together and we'll see where things go," he said.

When his mother shrieked with exhilaration, Gannon had to hold the phone away from his ear.

"That is absolutely wonderful. I can't wait to tell Millie that something is happening between you two."

"Ma, don't you dare. If you want me to ever tell you stuff again, you won't share anything I'm saying. Let the chips fall where they will. I'm enjoying being at the cabin and even more than that, I'm enjoying the time I'm spending with Danielle. It's been great and that's all I want to say about it. How are you doing? Dawn and Kris should be home today and I'm sure they'll be by to see you," he said.

"I just talked to them. They tried to convince me to not call and wake you up, but I told them it was almost noon and you would most likely be up even if your party ran late, which I'm sure it did."

"Yes, it ran late and yes I was already up and about to grab a shower and go for a run."

"Did your sister tell you Michelle came by the office looking for you? Any idea what she wants? I hope she's not trying to weasel her way back into your life. She was a deceitful woman who doesn't deserve a second chance. You know that, right?"

"I'm not looking to give her a second chance at anything. That's over and has been over for months. There's no going back."

"That's good to hear. I don't like how she lied to you for so long. I would hate for any of her antics to ruin what you and Danielle have," she said.

Gannon laughed again, loving how his mother took everything he said and ran with it, spinning it into what she wanted it to be.

"I didn't say there was anything happening with Danielle. I said I have been enjoying some time with her since we're both here at the lake. That's all I'm saying and that's all you should hear. Don't read more into it until I say there's more, okay?"

Gannon knew if he let his mother run wild and free, she would have him and Danielle getting married in a few days.

"I hear you. Wishful thinking, I guess. You know Millie and I always assumed we would be in-laws. Maybe we still can," she said.

"I'm hanging up now. I'm coming back to Georgia next week for the day for a meeting. I'll come by while I'm there."

"Perhaps you can bring Danielle with you and she can visit with me while you're at the office having your meeting."

"Mom!" he exclaimed.

"Okay, no need to fire any shots. I was just saying," she said.

Gannon laughed again.

"Did you just say something about shots being fired? I need you to stop watching Chicago, P.D. I know it's your favorite show, but you're picking up too much show jargon," he quipped.

"Think about it. I would love to see her."

"I'll think about it, mom. I love you and I'll see you at the end of next week."

Gannon disconnected the call and was about to put the phone done when he heard a chime signaling a text message. Reading it, he smiled.

"I guess after making love like two sex-starved

teenagers, the next move was for you to leave me with your cell phone number. I miss the warmth of your body already. I hope you're coming back later after picking up more necessities."

Gannon couldn't help but laugh and then remember their antics from the night before and earlier that morning. He made a mental note to stop at the local store for more condoms. It was clear they were on the same page that they hadn't gotten enough of each other.

He typed back a quick note.

"Good morning, beautiful. I'm already on it. Get some rest and I'll see you in a bit. I'm going for a run."

After seeing her emojis with smiles and kisses, he returned a few choice emojis and headed for the shower. He had a woman to get back to.

11

After a few laps in the pool, Gannon stepped out to find Danielle sitting on the edge waiting for him. Walking over to her, he leaned down and tasted her sweet lips, an act he was finding quite addicted.

After spending their first night together after his party a few days ago, they had spent the last three nights together either at his house or her house. It seemed neither enjoyed being in bed alone when they could be sharing a bed together.

Today, they woke and had gone for a bike ride, using bikes his family kept in their garage. Once they returned, he felt like cooling off from the heat of the day by going for a swim. When Danielle agreed to join him, he couldn't wait to see what bathing suit she would show up in. The first one, over a week ago, had been hot pink and it had him hot for her all day.

Today, she wore a two-piece yellow suit, just as hot and sexy as the pink one. She had a body that was meant for a two-piece suit and he loved seeing her in it. As soon as he finished his swim, he looked forward to taking it off of her succulent body.

"I needed that kiss," she said and stood to walk back into the house with him.

"That's good because I think I'm addicted to kissing you. You already know I can't get enough of making love to you," Gannon said, pulling her into his arms and kissing her more thoroughly this time, causing a sensual moan to escape from them both.

"You know, action works better than words," Danielle said and stepped out of his embrace. She saw the pained look on Gannon's face as she pulled away. That look turned to one of pure delight the moment she untied the top of her bathing suit and let it fall to the floor.

Gannon licked his lips knowing what was on the horizon. The minute her top hit the floor, his swim trunks seemed a little more snug than usual as his body rose to the occasion of what was next.

"I'm all about the action, baby," he said walking toward her. He smiled when she backed up out of his reach.

"Is that so?"

Danielle reached for the ties on each side of her hips and untied the bottom half. As it fell away, she let her eyes travel over his body and noticed the mushroom head of him sticking out over the band of his trunks.

"Looks to me like you need some bigger trunks because I wouldn't want that part of you to be smaller. That big boy is the perfect size for me," she slurred and then purred like a kitten.

"Then why are you backing away from me if you see

something you like!" he exclaimed and again moved toward her.

"Oh, I see something I like alright, but in order for you to get something you like, you have to catch me first," she said laughing.

Gannon removed his trunks and the moment they stood naked and watching each other to see who would move first, neither spoke as they individually planned their next move toward winning the battle.

Danielle laughed first and lost as she headed for the steps with him close behind her. Before she could make it to his bedroom, she felt her body being lifted into the air as Gannon picked her up and put her over his shoulder as she laughed uncontrollably until they reached the bed and fell onto it together.

Without moving, their eyes met and no words were exchanged as they let the moment sink in as if they knew it was by some miracle that they were together, something neither of them would take for granted.

"I've thought about you a lot over the years. I wondered if you were happy, if you missed me, if you even really loved me. I know we were young, but I loved you more than anything."

Gannon didn't want to keep bringing up the past, but he felt like something needed to be said. They had fallen back in step as if they had never parted ways years ago. It was easy because they never stopped caring about each other and here they were, wrestling around in bed.

Danielle reached up and caressed the lines of his goatee with her perfectly manicured, long painted nail and looked him in the eye without blinking.

"I thought about you all the time. I purposed goaded my mom into revealing details about you when I talked to her. I wanted to know that you were happy and hoped that you'd found love again, even if I did not. I thought it was love, but it wasn't. I was a love for the life I thought I would live. My heart always belonged to you, something I didn't realize until after I got married. I should have walked away then, but at that time, pride wouldn't allow me to. My family was hurt by my decision to drop out of school, without telling them. For months, they thought I was at school and I was living in California. The pain in my mom and dad's voice is what kept me away, something I was ashamed about. I loved you, Gannon, more than anything and I don't know what I was thinking. I guess I really wasn't."

"What about now?"

Gannon searched her face and felt her pain. She was still carrying the weight of her choice.

"Now, I'm afraid to think that this is anything but real. I never thought I would be here with you like this, but I am. I'm praying that this is the beginning of finding our way back to each other. This isn't any kind of rebound thing, if that's what you're thinking. I want you and only you."

"I want you and only you, too. I can't say that I've

waited all these years for you, but I've loved you. Perhaps, my marriage didn't work out, not only because of what she did, but because I may not have given one hundred percent to it like I should have. You were always a part of me. Being with you now, I know that you always will be a part of me."

Danielle wanted to cry with jubilance, but she didn't. Instead, she kissed him, slow and methodically, taking great care to express all the love she had for him with the way she caressed his lips with hers.

Rolling Danielle under him, Gannon knew no more words were needed. He had what he needed knowing that they were always meant to be together and he no longer wanted to live in the past of what should have been. He wanted to live in the here and now of what is and what will be.

Putting protection in place, he joined their bodies and allowed the love to flow between them, shutting out the world and reclaiming their place in each other's lives. As he made passionate love to her, loving and stoking the fires that were burning hot between them, he gave her every part of him, not just the physical. He gave her his heart knowing that this time, she would cherish it forever.

"I'm whole when I'm with you," Danielle whispered in Gannon's ear as her body moved with a rhythm that matched his stroke for stroke. She needed him to know that she was all in and wanted everything he had to give.

"I need you, baby. I've always needed you," Gannon groaned out.

"You have me – all of me."

Danielle tried to prolong the moment, but the love that flowed from him to her and back to him was too powerful to ignore or hold back.

Gannon, with an extra burst of energy inhaled the essence of the moment and a smell as sweet as ambrosia seared through him, ascending from her body engulfed him as he crooned his heightened desire for her over and over while his body jackknifed uncontrollably as Danielle moved in an in sync, uncontrollable pace with him. Arching his back to add more to their lovemaking, he got an unerring feeling of exactly what she needed and with precise piston-like strokes, she screamed and gave into the pleasure that coursed through them both as an orgasm ripped through him and her and they savored the ultimate intimate pleasure a man and woman could have.

**

Lying in bed in each other's arms, the only sound either of them heard were of the sounds of the crickets outside of the window. Gannon had no problem with the fact that for the past three hours, they lay like this, content with knowing the world, right now, consisted of them and nothing or no one else.

"I feel complete in your arms," Danielle said. "Everything about us feels right. Is it just me?" she added.

"No, baby. It's not just you. It's a mutual feeling. This moment is absolutely perfect," he said nuzzling her neck.

"I never want to leave this room."

Gannon chuckled. "We have to leave sometime. Eventually we'll need sustenance."

"Okay, I'm willing to leave it for food, but then we must come right back."

"Deal! I forgot, I have to leave on Friday, so I guess I'll have to go back on the what I just agreed to. I'm driving into Georgia on Friday for the day and will most likely stay the night and come back sometime Saturday. Would you like to go? I need to stop by the office for a meeting and thought you might like a tour?"

"Really? You won't mind me tagging along?"

"Well, I am asking you because I want you along."

"I would love a tour of the factory where the baby food is made. Your company's food is what I hear every parent talking about, especially those who want to feed their babies only organic food. The fact that you offer options appeals to the masses. One day when I have children, I'll be buying your whole line of baby food."

Gannon didn't know how to respond to that. He saw them having and raising kids together. He didn't know if Danielle's comment was meant to have him thinking in a different direction. He wanted to know if they were on the same page.

"Turn toward me," he said and gave her room to turn over.

"What's wrong?" she asked when she saw the sad look on his face.

"Nothing's wrong. I love you and I wanted you to know that."

Danielle stopped breathing and had to catch herself to exhale and not hold her breath. Gannon Wilcox had said words she never thought she'd hear again.

"I love you, too."

"Are you sure?" he asked.

"Yes. I've never, ever been surer of anything more than the fact that I love you with everything in me."

"Good. When you talk about having babies and buying baby food, I want you thinking in terms of you and I having babies and feeding them baby food from our company."

Danielle got it and could slap herself.

"I said it didn't I? It sounded like I wasn't thinking long term about us. Gannon, you are it for me and I never, ever want another man that isn't you. I messed up our lives once by not doing the right thing and I will never do that again. I love you and all I want is you and one day your beautiful babies," she said, gleaming knowing that he wanted a future with her as much as she wanted one with him.

12

"Are you sure your mom wants to see me?" Danielle asked as they pulled up to park in front of his mother's house.

After getting a tour of the company, Gannon sprung on her that they were going to stop at his mother's house before taking in a movie and having dinner later that evening. She was happy that his sisters had been receptive to her presence at the lake and around him once again, but mothers were different.

"Yes, she asked specifically to see you and she was happy about it. Why? What's wrong?"

Gannon turned toward her and removed the key from the ignition.

Danielle bit her bottom lip to stifle her nervousness. She wasn't sure he knew how his mother really felt about her and even she wasn't sure. She did have a feeling it wasn't good.

"I'm not as sure as you are that your mother wanting to see me is a good thing. Did you know after I ended our relationship, your mother told my mother that I was the cause of you staying away from the lake for years when you came home on leave? She blamed me that you avoided the lake so that you wouldn't run into me and your family suffered the loss of your presence when they were there. I don't think she just decided to forget all about that and welcome me with open arms."

"My sisters did," he stated.

"I know and I'm glad they did. Sisters are not mothers."

Gannon reached over and took her hands in his.

"Listen, my mother is not like that. She may have been angry back then and that's because she knew how hurt I was. I got over it and I'm sure she did, too. Life is too short to hold grudges and no one knows that better than my mom. Even before my dad passed away, she embraced life like every day was her last day. She doesn't have a mean bone in her body. Trust me, it'll be okay. Come on," he said getting out of the car.

Danielle inhaled and exhaled loudly to douse the nervousness she didn't want to show once inside the house. When Gannon opened the door and smiled at her, she relaxed, trusting him that visiting his mother would be okay.

"If you're sure it's okay."

Gannon leaned down and kissed her sweetly.

"Relax and trust me that it's fine."

Danielle placed her hand in his and walked with

him to the house.

"Mom!" Gannon said using his key to let them in the house.

"I'm in the kitchen!" she hollered back.

As they walked to the back of the house, Danielle walked a few steps behind him. When they reached the kitchen, he pulled her in front of him. There went her idea to stay in his shadow and out of the line of fire.

"I smell something good," Gannon said.

He tried to look at what his mother was bent over trying to retrieve from the oven.

"I knew you were coming, so I baked a pie! That sounds like a corny line from a movie," she said. Placing the pie on the stove, she turned around.

"Why, hello!" she said directly to Danielle.

"Hi, Ms. Anna. It's good to see you."

Danielle stood in the safety of Gannon's embrace until she saw his mother open her arms to her for a hug. Without any hesitation, she walked around the kitchen counter and into her embrace.

"It's wonderful to see you, too. Gannon told me you were coming into town with him and I was hoping you would have time to stop by. How's the family?" she asked.

"Everyone is great. You look wonderful!" Danielle said.

"Hello? I'm here, too!" Gannon declared.

He raised his hands in surrender when his mother

jokingly smirked at him.

"Son, you know I love seeing you, but it's been years since I've seen Danielle, in person that is."

Danielle tried not to let the embarrassed look show on her face. Lots of people didn't see her in person, but the world got a front seat view of her life in the media.

"I'm just saying, can your son get a hug, too?" he asked and playfully pushed Danielle to the side and embraced his mother with a hug and a slight lift from the floor. When she giggled, he sat her back down on her feet.

"You're so dramatic. Since you're here and feeling energetic, can you get the lawn furniture out of the shed. If you have a little extra energy, you can power wash it for me. The hose is already connected. Danielle and I can relax, catch up and enjoy some of this hot pie. I'll save half the pie for you to take with you," she said.

"Anything for you," he said looking at Danielle who had a look in her eyes that said she was afraid for him to leave her alone. "I'll be out back if either of you need me," he said directly to her, but spoke to them both.

After he exited the house through the kitchen sliding glass doors, Danielle stood uncomfortably as she watched Gannon's mother move around the kitchen getting plates and a knife to cut the pie.

"I hope you still love fresh apple pie from scratch. I

picked these apples from my own garden out back."

"Yes, I love apple pie and you always did make the best."

"Good, have a seat and I'll get us a slice and some lemonade."

"Can I help with anything?" she asked.

"Why don't you get the lemonade from the refrigerator and then sit at the table."

Doing so and sitting at the table, Danielle waited.

Anna sat across from her and she hoped she couldn't sense her uneasiness.

"The pie smells wonderful."

"You know you can relax. You look uncomfortable and you shouldn't be."

"I'm sorry. I admit, I was nervous about being here. It's been a lot of years since I've seen you and the last time wasn't the best. I apologize for that," she said with heartfelt emotion.

"Why are you apologizing? For what happened between you and my son back then? Clearly, it's not a problem for the two of you anymore and it never really was for me. I felt for my son's misery back then, but he was a man and learned how to deal with it."

"You're not still angry about the way I hurt him?"

"Child, you and my son were young back then, maintaining a relationship that wasn't ready to be in play yet, if that makes sense. I reacted as any mother would when someone hurts one of their children and that's called human nature. It was a human reaction to a situation."

"My mother told me how angry you were."

"I was and after I expressed my feelings about it, I let it go."

Danielle poured the lemonade and inhaled the smell of the pie that was placed in front of her. Apple pie was her favorite of all pies and one thing she remembered was her freshly baked pies and without an invitation to do so, she picked up her fork and took her first bite."

"This is so good," she said.

"I love when people enjoy my food."

"Back then, I didn't have any real direction in my life. That's not to slight my parents, but once I went away to school, I lost focus of what was important. I reacted hastily and it didn't take long for regret to set in, but by then, I had already made so many bad mistakes, including eloping with Blain and there was no coming back from that."

"You let that embarrassment keep you away from your family for years. Gannon did the same thing, using the military as an excuse to stay away. Our families were so close, it would have been hard for you both to be around not knowing if the other would be around or not. For two years, neither one of you came around. Gannon finally did again once he got married."

"I thought about him all the time, what he was doing, how life turned out for him. When I talked to my mom, she would tell me he seemed happy while I was in California being miserable. My life with Gannon on the lake, even though we were young, were the best times of my life. He loves hard and he wears his heart on his sleeve."

"He always has and that made him vulnerable. It also made him a perfect catch for a woman who appreciates the wonderful man he is. Is that you now?" Anna asked and looked across the table to look Danielle in the eye.

"Yes, it is."

"Do you know why I wanted to talk to you?" she asked.

"No, ma'am."

"I love my son and his happiness, like my daughters' is most important to me. My life with my husband was not always a perfect one, but it was filled with love, honor and respect. He was a hard-working man, but we agreed early in our marriage that we would place each other and our family first. We built that house on the lake as a place to escape the world and focus on love and family. There are executives of companies who never take time away from their companies to spend weeks away on family trips, but my husband did that. My son is a lot like him because he values family, though he loves running the company now. Deep down, he wants more than just the company. His first wife didn't want the same things and it was obvious to all of us, but Gannon. He focused on loving her and giving her whatever she wanted, but that wasn't a two-way street. She took and took. I know my son and he has fallen for you again. I wanted to see you and talk to you, so that I could see for myself who you have become."

"I love Gannon," Danielle admitted. "I'm in love with him," she added.

"I know and he still loves you. I don't think he ever stopped. Did he ever tell you how I met his father?"

"No, he never did."

"Before there were houses on that lake, it was a campground many, many years ago. I was from Georgia, but my husband was from Maryland. A lot of local summer camps would take advantage of two-week trips to that camping area with tons of cabins that were spread out. There was a large fence that kept kids safely away from the water's edge. One summer when I was fifteen, the same age you were when you and Gannon became a couple, I met his father there. For a week, we eyed one another, but played like we didn't like each other for the sake of our friends. Boys were worse at it in order to keep some image with their friends."

Danielle laughed.

"Gannon was like that around his friends around that age. Boys, huh?" she exclaimed.

"They all do it. The first day of the second week, they finally let us swim in the lake, so that gate was opened and all of the kids from all of the camps descended on the lake. Everyone, but me, that is. I didn't know how to swim. Gerald would act like he didn't want to swim and would sit on the water's edge with me. We would talk until they made us go back to the campground. We did that for the entire week. By the time we left to go back home that summer, we were in love. We may have been fifteen, but we were in love, so I understood when Gannon proclaimed he was in love with you at that age. Sitting on that lake every day talking to Gerald were the best times of my childhood. Those two weeks were everything. He told me one day that he would build a house on a lake just like that and he would marry me, but first I had to learn how to swim."

"You did learn because I remember watching you swim as if you had been doing it your whole life," Danielle said.

"I did. When school started and we could choose an elective, I chose swimming. Gerald and I would write each other and stay in contact and that next summer when we went to camp, I was one of the first ones to jump in that lake. He was so proud of me. We made the best of those two weeks. We would sit on the water's edge or the pier, which was an older one back then, not the newer one that's there now and we would talk about everything. We would dream together, tune out the entire world and focus on the two of us. We knew we were going to get married one day and Gerald talked about all of the things he needed to do to make sure we had a good life. He eventually went to college, I went to college and we stayed a committed couple. On our breaks each summer, we would meet for a few weeks in North Carolina and spend time at the lake. After graduating, he proposed to me right on that lake and I accepted. We spent a few years struggling to make our dreams happen and then the baby food business came about when he used old recipes passed down to him from his grandmother and mother which is when the business started making really good money. We were then living in Georgia and he was able to build an even larger factory than the small one he'd been operating out of. One day, I discovered I was pregnant and I wanted to tell him at what we called, our lake. We took a ride up there and saw a sign that the camp was no longer going to operate and the land had been sold to a developer who was interested in families who were looking to build homes on the property. We were one of the first buyers and so were your parents."

"Really? That is so amazing and so romantic. I never knew you met your husband there," Danielle said, still nipping away at her pie, but found it hard to do anything but focus on the story.

"That lake is a special place and we've always told our kids how we met and fell in love there. When the same thing happened to Gannon, it was amazing to see your love blossom as ours did and if you remember, we never tried to keep you apart. My husband and I knew the magic of how love blooms on the lake."

Danielle looked down.

"Then I ruined everything," she said somberly.

Anna reached over and raised Danielle's face until they were eye level again.

"I had to understand that what the lake was for my husband and I didn't have to be the same for Gannon, though it started out that way."

"We were in love. I've never loved anyone like I loved and still love Gannon. I messed up everything we could have been."

"Maybe so, but who is to say everything that happened wasn't a part of the plan all along. I'm going to tell you something I haven't even told Gannon or anyone else. Before my husband passed away, we talked about our children's happiness and he said one day, you and Gannon would get married and have lots of little babies and that his only regret was that he wouldn't live long enough to see that happen. He wanted to so much, but God had another plan. I wasn't as big of a believer as he was, but he was adamant about what he knew. He told me to look hard at the life you were living because it was all over the news channels. He said that wasn't the life you were meant to live. At that time, Gannon was separated from his wife who was a liar and schemer. Gerald would say it was all a part of the plan. Not all marriages start out and follow the path mine and his did. He believed one day, the lake would draw you both back to it and you would remember how you fell in love and what real, true love felt like. That would be when the lifetime of love you're supposed to have together would begin. When I heard you were at the lake and Gannon was there, I remembered what Gerald said. I wanted to see you to tell you that story because I don't want there to be any regret or remorse in you over something that happened years ago. Today is today and when I turned and saw the two of you standing in my kitchen with his arms around you, I knew Gerald had been right."

Danielle tried to hold back the tears that fell from her eyes, but couldn't.

"I needed to hear that. I couldn't believe my eyes when I opened my door and Gannon was standing on the other side of it. The moment I drove up to the lake, he was all I could think about and then the next day, there he was. I remember all the things we talked about and dreamed of when we were young and all the beauty that was the lake, has always lived in me. I spent too much time away from family and the lake and when I got there, it was as if the lake was saying welcome back to your life the way it was supposed to be. Then there was Gannon."

"Sweetheart, I can't foretell the future, but I will say if you and my son were able to find your way back to each other while on the lake, trust what's in your heart. I love my son and whatever makes him happy is what I want for him. If that's you, I'm happier than you know. I am a testimony that life is too short to live in the past. Live each day with purpose."

"Can I have some pie now?" Gannon asked entering the kitchen and seeing a moment between his mother and Danielle. He wondered what happened.

"Yes, you can."

Anna stood after giving Danielle's hand a comforting squeeze, a sign to let her know everything would be fine.

Danielle turned, wiped her eyes and turned back to him.

"This pie is the best pie I've ever eaten. You better come get you some or I'm going to eat the whole thing."

Gannon walked over to the table and sat down.

"Is everything okay in here?" he asked seeing unshed tears in her eyes.

She looked at him and smiled.

"Everything is perfect. You have no idea how perfect it is."

"She's right, now eat so you're not late for your movie," Anna said and walked out of the kitchen, grinning. Everything was back on track. Gerald had predicted the day would come when she would see her son happy, in love and with Danielle again.

As she walked toward the sitting room where she and Gerald spent most of their time, she looked up and talked directly to him as if he could hear her.

"You were right. The lake is again working its magic," she said, sat down, crossed her legs and took in the moment of jubilee knowing life was again as it should have always been.

13

Danielle woke to find Gannon standing on the side of the bed with a tray in his hand.

"You're up early," she said, yawning.

"I'm anxious to get back to the lake. We have a six-hour drive ahead of us."

"I was sure after making love all night long, you would be as tired as I am," she said smiling and sitting up.

"Making love to you doesn't exhaust me, it invigorates me. I'm anxious to get out of this work environment. The few hours I was in the office, everyone wanted my undivided attention as if I'm never coming back," he joked.

"Your team loves and respects you. It's like a family around there. I loved the tour and talking to everyone. What is this company cookout I heard about? I understand you pay for all the employees and their families to come together?"

"I do. It's a tradition my father started many years ago. It's one of the few times each year that he completely shuts down production. At the end of the summer, he always paid for a day of fun with food and games and it's the hit of the year. I think they thought I wasn't going to continue it, but I plan to keep everything the way my dad had it."

"You are a remarkable man," she said. Danielle looked at the full plate of food in front of her. "Who is going to eat all of this?" she asked seeing scrambled eggs, toast, bacon, waffles and fresh fruit.

"I knew you would be tired. I kept you up all night and I wanted to give you a relaxed morning and a good meal before we left. I hope you enjoyed hanging with me."

"I did and I'm looking forward to heading back to the lake. I miss it already, though this house makes me want to stay forever. I love it, especially the view of the night sky from your bedroom. Last night was like making love under the stars. Do you always keep the curtains open at night?"

"I do because I love the night sky. I'm a dreamer and looking up through the skylight or through the large window allows me to focus."

"You've always been a dreamer. I've always loved that about you. Are you eating?" she asked.

"Yes. I thought we'd share yours."

"Great idea," Danielle said handing him the other fork on the tray.

"Are you going to tell me what happened between you and my mom yesterday? When I came in, you looked like you had been crying, but things didn't seem tense."

"I was crying and it wasn't a tense situation. We had a great talk. I mean it was wonderful and if you're okay with it, I don't want to share it. I don't want to keep secrets or complicate things, but she shared some things with me that I will forever cherish."

Gannon smiled and kissed her lips.

"I'm more than fine with that as long as you're okay. I know you were hesitant to go in the house."

Danielle smiled, remembering and inwardly rejoicing at the moment of bonding they shared.

"I was and I was cautious for no reason at all. I realize talking to your mother is exactly what I needed, just like having you in my life is exactly what I needed. So much time has passed and so many things have happened, but we're here. You and I are here and if there was ever a time in my life to be thankful, that time is now. I don't know that I'd be this happy right now if I hadn't gone to the lake house for some time to think. I don't want to think about not being there when you knocked on the door thinking my parents were there. I've thought about you over the years and I've never told anyone this, but I've wished a time or two that I could go back and change a lot of the choices I made, the main one being leaving you. Even since being back on the lake, I've thought that and wondered how happy we could have been building our lives together from that time."

Gannon moved the tray and pulled Danielle into his lap.

"Baby, we can't go back and I'm not so sure I would want to. It was a trying time and who knows what I would have done if the military didn't keep me busy for those eight years. I didn't make a lot of good choices either, but the best choice I ever made was taking my father's advice. Before he died, he told me I needed time to myself at the lake house. For a year after, I couldn't find the strength to go there because I wasn't ready to deal with the impact of him no longer being there with me to fish and have man talks. When I told him I didn't think I could do it, he said it was imperative that I did. He said my entire future depended on me going up to the lake house and letting go of everything that stood in the way of me moving on with my life. He often talked about the magic of that place and what it meant to him and the happiness he had there since he was fifteen years old. He knew I was separated from my ex-wife and what I was going through and he said one day, when I was ready, I would find the answer to everything I wanted in life right there on the lake."

He turned Danielle so that she straddled his lap and they could look eye to eye.

"Everything revolves around the lake," she whispered and kissed him sweetly.

"It does and it wasn't a coincidence that when I decided to go back to the lake, you were there. You, the person I have loved since I was a teenager was there. Neither of us were married anymore and we both were looking for guidance of what's next. I've found it and I hope you have, too," he said.

"When I said I was anxious to get back to the lake, it's not just about the lake, but it's also about us. I lost something years ago on that lake and in order for me to not only find, but keep what I hope I'm getting a second chance at, I need to be there and I need to be there with you. I love you, Gannon. I want to dream with you on our lake. I don't know what's down the road, but if it's a life with you in any way possible, I want that and I don't want any distractions."

"Tell me what you want? I'm not talking about me loving you because that's a given. What do you want to do with your life now? I know you have money and you can pretty much do whatever you want, but in your heart, what is it that you want the most?" he asked.

Danielle had been thinking about that and knew what the priority was.

"I want to finish school. That's the first thing I want to do. I know I told you that was on my list of things, but that's my priority. I have one year left and I'm going to enroll in school. After that, I want to get my cosmetology license and actually open my own salon and spa. I want something that's mine. That's a dream unfulfilled and it's time I did something about it. I want to spend the rest of the summer at the lake with you for as long as you'll be there. I know you love me and I love you, something I will never ever, ever take for granted again. I learned about love on that lake and I want to get back to the kind of love I was supposed to experience – with you. What about you? What do you want besides my love which, like you said, is a given?" she asked, smiling brightly.

Never again would she doubt what was meant to be.

"Besides wanting you, I want to finish school and expand the baby food brand. My sisters have a lot of great ideas and I'm planning on watching them put them into play. I know that I don't have to run the business alone because I have two sisters who are willing and able and with them alongside me at the helm, we'll all have time for more than just running the company. That's something my father wanted us to see. He ran the company, but every single summer, he was on the lake with us, making time for himself and us. I'm glad the business is successful, but that's not all life should be about. I want what my parents had and what your parents have. I want to one day have the life we are meant to have and have so many babies, people will think we have our own baseball team," he laughed.

"Yes, to babies and to love! Now, you know we don't have to have the babies today, but I would love to continue practicing at least one more time before we head back up to the lake."

Placing her arms behind Gannon's head, Danielle brought his mouth up to hers, tasting him and enjoying the delightful feeling that flowed through her loving the feel of being in his arms.

"Your pleasure is my command, baby," he said, pulling the nightshirt over her head and while pushing the tray of food further on the other side of the bed, he turned until she was under him. Each time they came together, they were placing a seal on their love, a love that was always meant to be.

14

Danielle's eyes were tired after spending hours searching the internet on how to re-enroll in college to complete her business management degree to begin the task of learning how to run and manage her own business. She had already inquired about going to cosmetology school and her excitement led her to laying out her plan for the next two years.

For the first time in years, she was following a path that was about her and no one else. She was thankful for the support Gannon gave her as soon as she began focusing on her next move. That was the reason she came to the lake, to focus on that. She now had even more of a reason to rejoice because she was back with him and life couldn't be more perfect.

While she spent the day focusing on research, Gannon had gone on a few errands, giving her time to work on something other than finding more reasons to be naked, something she loved. Her body shuttered with a minor quake at the thought of how perfectly they connected on an intimate level. He was the kind of man that made a woman appreciate being naked with him all the time and outside of the bedroom, they were good for each other and they had each other's backs, something that was needed to keep a relationship strong. Her family always stood behind her even after making all the wrong moves, but her fear of admitting she was wrong in choosing Blain kept her in an unhappy, unhealthy place and with a man who never thought she could be more than a pretty face. She wasn't moving on with her life and planning out her career to prove anything to him or anyone else, she was doing it for herself.

She was glad to be free of a man who never considered her an equal. Though he had been trying to reach her for the past few weeks, she kept her promise to herself to break all ties with him. Hungry, she got up to eat when there was a knock at the front door. It couldn't be Gannon, because he always used the back door. Going to check, she huffed in frustration at the face she saw looking back at her through the peephole. Blain.

She snatched the door open and let her dislike for him being at her door show on her face and in her body language.

"What are you doing here and how did you know I was here?" she asked.

"Aren't you going to let me in? You should have a better greeting than that for your husband."

"No, I'm not inviting you in and you shouldn't be here. I told you many times already that we have nothing to talk about and you shouldn't be here."

"I'm here because you're here. You weren't taking any of my calls and I even emailed you and you didn't respond. Then last week, I called you and your number had changed. I've been checking everywhere for you, the two properties and everywhere else I thought you'd go and nothing. On a whim, I tried the lake house wondering if you were here. I remember you saying it was a great place to think."

"You never cared about the lake or my ability to think. Why now?" she asked boldly.

"I love you, Danielle. I know I haven't always shown it the right way, but I do, now invite me in and let's talk."

When Blain tried to walk around her to get inside, she pushed him back.

"You're not coming and we have nothing to talk about. Our life together is over. I saw the news report last week where two women presented paternity test results and you're the father. Why would you think I would want to come back to that drama? There is nothing for me to go back to and I would never even think about it."

Blain stood back and gave her a once over. She knew he was trying to figure out why she wasn't giving into him like she had in the past.

"There's someone else. I see it. You're involved with someone. Well, ain't that something," he said glumly.

"What I do with my personal life is none of our

business. Go back to Hollywood, to your lifestyle for the rich and famous. None of that is for me and it never was. I've moved on completely and you need to stop reaching out to me. I'm not interested, nor will I ever be. Goodbye."

Danielle wanted to slam the door in his face, but she didn't feel the need to be petty. Blain was her past and there was no need for anger. Instead of slamming the door, she closed it slowly as he stood stunned that he didn't get his usual reaction from her. She hoped the closing of the door showed him that the life they shared at one time was now a closed subject.

Going back into the kitchen, she focused on getting something to eat and smiled knowing she'd finally taken her life back.

**

Gannon drove back to the lake with everything he needed for a romantic dinner with Danielle, including fresh roses he looked forward to giving her. They had been back from visiting his mother for a week and in that time, they listened to each other's plans and where they wanted their lives to be. Earlier in the day, he'd focused on enrolling back in school for the semester that would start in a few weeks in order to finally finish his degree. He set up some conference calls with his sisters about ideas to expand the business and he was just as excited to help Danielle with the plans for her next move.

Life was great and going in the right direction. He

couldn't be happier until his phone rang and he saw the name on the screen.

"Michelle, I heard you've been trying to reach me," he said answering.

"You've been avoiding me, Gannon. I've called your cell several times and I've even stopped by your office. I was told you were away for a few weeks. I hope everything is okay," she said.

"Everything is fine. I'm surprised to hear from you."

"I know I probably shocked you by being so adamant about speaking to you. I've been thinking about you and I was hoping we could talk, in person."

"Talk about what?"

"About how I'm not sure we gave our marriage an honest try."

"Really? Was that before or after you failed to tell me you were on birth control when we were supposed to be trying to have a baby?"

Gannon wasn't falling for any tricks or games. What they had was over.

"I know and I was wrong for that. We loved each other and with counseling, we should have been able to work out our problems. Did we really give it our all? Did we give it an honest try?"

"What happened? Did you find that the grass wasn't greener on the other side? I heard you were seeing someone and know who that someone is, I'm assuming you realized life with me looked pretty good. It's not happening, Michelle. We weren't meant for each other or there would not have been deceit, lying and scheming. I would appreciate it if you didn't go by the company any more and please, don't call me anymore. Truly, love doesn't live here anymore for us. I wish you the best that life has to offer, but trust me, it isn't me."

Gannon didn't wait for her to respond before disconnecting the call. He'd said all he needed to say and was through going back to the past. He wanted it to stay where it was, in his rear-view mirror. Pulling up to his house, he hopped out and raced to put the bags in the house before going over to check on Danielle.

Coming back out to the car, thinking he'd left something, he instead walked across the front of the house and knocked on Danielle's front door.

Shocking him, the door flew open and Danielle's face was a stern scowl, causing him to step back.

"Whoa? What's wrong?" he asked.

"Oh, I'm sorry. I thought you were someone else," he said and needed to feel a connection, she went into his arms, wrapping her tightly around his waist.

"Tell me what's going on? Who did you think I was?"

"Blain."

"Blain? Why would I be Blain?"

"He was here," she said with her face pressed closely to his chest. The minute she felt Gannon's arms pull her closer, she held on for dear life.

"Yes, and I thought you were him coming back. You never use the front door."

"I was getting bags from the car and walked right over to tell you I was going to cook us a marvelous dinner tonight. Are you alright? Did he hurt you or anything?"

Danielle moved back so that he could see that she was okay.

"I'm fine and no he didn't. I was surprised to see him show up here unexpectedly, but he's gone now. I told him off in a polite way and I'm sure he's gone for good."

"What did he want?"

"Me."

"Explain."

The last thing Gannon expected was to see or hear anything about Blain, not anymore.

"He showed up wanting me to give our marriage another try as if I would actually do that."

"What made him leave?"

"He could see that I was happy and he rightly assumed I was seeing someone. He hadn't see me looing happy in a long time and probably not in all the time we were together."

"Must be a full moon kind of day. My ex called me today and I gave her the final boot, too. She thought we could give our marriage another try."

Danielle laughed. She was glad the moment was tense between them. There was nothing like an old ex coming into a new situation to screw things up.

"Looks like they both can see that we're great catches," she joked.

"Only for each other. They are both water under the bridge. Now, thinking about everything other than either one of them, what do you say to lobster dinners, with grilled shrimp and asparagus by candlelight?"

"I say bring it on. This time is about me and you."

"I agree because the lake is saying so," he laughed and kissed her deeply.

15

Excitement was in the air as Gannon tried hard to not let too much of it show or Danielle would assume something was up and though it was, he didn't want her to know about it. They had been together on the lake for the past three months, with him taking the occasional trip down to Georgia, some with and without her, so that he could check in with his family and the company. Things were going well and since he hadn't planned on being away from the office as long as he had, after being there for several weeks, he'd had all of the electronic equipment he would need to conduct work from the lake house delivered and installed in the house. He turned the extra guest room into an office, which allowed him to not feel as disconnected.

He and Danielle had registered for classes which would be starting in a few days and they decided to move together into his house back in Georgia.

His sisters had come up a few times along with their planning and marketing teams and they worked on how to expand the brand. Most excitedly, the last time they came up for a few days, they brought their mother with them and even though their father wasn't with them, it felt good having everyone around again. No one dwelled on the fact that he and Danielle had practically moved into his family's lake house together. It was as if everyone expected that to be the next step.

As they prepared for the end of the summer at the lake, they'd gotten up early in the morning to take the boat out on the open water. For most of the summer, they spent time on it right on the lake, but he had a reason for needing her away from the lake house for the day. They had one more hour before he needed to head back to the pier.

"I don't want this summer to end," Danielle said coming up behind him as he lay out on the deck. She had been preparing their lunch of grilled salmon and steamed vegetables.

"I know how you feel, but I'm excited for what's next for us both. Look at us going back to school and finishing our degrees and soon we'll both be entrepreneurs running businesses."

Danielle sat the food down as she slid the cooler of bottled water and wine coolers closer to them.

"Are you concerned that all these plans we're making will interfere with our time together? I don't want anything to come between our love, especially not business," she admitted.

"Baby, nothing is going to come before our love. If

we've learned nothing else, it's to make sure we put each other first and we'll continue to do that. Anytime we need a break, we'll hop in the truck and make our way here to the lake and rediscover any part of our love that we've taken for granted."

Danielle sat down beside him and he pulled her close.

"The other weekend when my parents were here visiting, my dad told me he was proud of me and that he never wanted to hear me talk about the mistakes I've made in the past. He said I have him and mom and your parents as examples of what true love is all about and it's about sacrificing so that family and love were a priority. I want to be sure you're my priority. I don't want chasing dreams to get in the way of that," she explained.

"Nothing and I mean nothing will get in the way. The one thing you have never really done is chased your own dreams and I don't care what they are, I am going to be beside you making them come true. We are in this together. Anything you want to do, any achievement you want to strive for, you share it with me and we're going after it. I love you and what we have isn't about me or you, it's about us together. Together we can be a powerful couple and we don't have to put our dreams aside to do that. We have to remember how much we love each other and make each other our priority. I have no doubt we're going to do that, so don't worry your pretty little head about anything. Have I told you how incredible you look in that white two-piece bathing suit? You are a walking fashion magazine. Everything you wear makes me believe you should be on a runway."

"I love how you encourage me with everything you say. I had one idea along that line that I was thinking about, but I didn't know how crazy it would sound."

Danielle pulled out their plates as Gannon began filling their plates with food while they talked.

"Nothing is crazy coming out of your sweet, delectable mouth. Let me hear it," he said.

"I was actually thinking about creating my own line of lingerie and bathing suit attire. I love sexy clothing, something you've noticed," she said with a sexy look on her face.

Gannon looked her up and down and whistled.

"Yeah, I've noticed. Anything on that body would be hard to miss," he acknowledged.

"I'm thinking of taking some of the money I have and investing it in designing and creating my own line. What do you think about that?" she asked.

"I think it's a great idea and definitely if you're using your body to model them. I'll take a front row seat to anything you want to test out on me!" he quipped and moved when Danielle reached over to swing lovingly at him.

"The way you look at me, I feel so sexy."

"I mean it and I'm serious about the idea. What do you need? Let's make it happen," Gannon said.

"Well, I have ideas about the style and colors, but I need someone who is actually good at design and marketing."

"I have a great idea. You should partner up with my sister. She's the one with the marketing degree and she can probably connect you with some designers who are starting out and will want to work with you."

"You think she'll want to do it?"

"Dawn would love to do it. She's been talking about a line of baby clothes to go along with the baby food line. She thought about that with all of the babies around that we use as models. We borrow the clothes and she's been talking for years about developing and marketing our own line of clothes. When we get back to town, set something up with her."

Danielle tried to hide her excitement, but she was elated at the thought of creating things that were hers.

"I will do that. We are going to be that powerful couple, aren't we?" she asked.

"We are. I'm telling you, it's this lake. It's as if everything we want and need in life, this lake reveals to us the direction to go in even when it comes to love because you, my love, are my everything. I fell in love with you on this lake and we rediscovered that love here on this lake."

"I'm glad our parents had the idea of building houses on this lake. I can't wait for the many more plans we'll make from this place."

"Let's eat up so we can get back. We need to get

packed up and then take time to get your things moved into our house."

Danielle grinned.

"It is going to be our house isn't it?" she asked.

"It already is. We just have to physically get you into it."

"I'm ready for that."

**

Pulling the boat up to the pier, Gannon looked toward the house hoping everything was ready. While Danielle was down below cleaning everything up and packing from their day out, he grabbed his cell phone and sent Dawn a short text. He waited a few seconds for her confirmation and smiled when she replied with a thumbs-up.

"Are you ready?" Danielle asked coming up with bags in her hand.

"I am. I'm going to call Mike to come and pick the boat up next weekend. Dawn is coming up next week and that'll be it for the season.

"Our time here has been magical and though I will miss it, I'm ready for the next phase in our life, happy that it'll be together."

Gannon pulled her into his arms, embracing her through the pink top and denim shorts she slipped over her bathing suit. He had also slipped on cargo shorts and a t-shirt. Knowing what was waiting for them, they need clothes on.

"Our next phase is going to be our best phase. Let's

get everything up to the house," he said.

For the first time in a long time, Gannon felt anxious as they walked toward the house. He hadn't been this nervous even when he took over the reins of the company from his father. He was also happiest about where life was about to take them. As they reached the stairs that led to the deck, he turned to Danielle who was a few steps behind him.

"I forgot my cell phone. Give me your bag and I'll take it in with all of these. Can you run and grab my phone? It's right near the main controls," he said.

"Anything for you, boo!" Danielle exclaimed, sitting her bag down at the bottom of the steps and turned to head back toward the boat.

Gannon took the bag and made haste to get inside of the house and waited.

Danielle looked around and saw Gannon's phone sitting right where he said it would be. As she walked back toward the house, she saw that he was already inside and hopefully lighting the fireplace for one of their last romantic nights on the lake. Nothing in the world could make her happier than she was at the moment. Life couldn't get any better.

As she walked up on the deck and slid the glass door back, she entered the darkened house and wondered why Gannon hadn't turned on a light. Reaching for the switch by the door, she turned and was startled, causing her to shriek. She took in the scene before her and would have said something, but no words would come out.

Looking around, she locked eyes with first her mother and father who stood beaming at her with joy. Next to them stood her sister and her family and shockingly, her brother was also there. Next to them stood Gannon's mother, his sisters Dawn and Kris and their families.

"What, what are you all doing here? Where is Gannon?" she said looking around for him.

"I'm right here, baby," he said and walked into the room from the kitchen. In his hands he held a large bouquet of red, white, yellow and orange roses. "I'm right here," he said again.

"What is all this?" she said as her voice shook.

"This is me making sure our life is on a path to being everything we want it to be and doing it together. I have our families here today, thanks to my sister who coordinated getting everyone here at this precise moment because I want them here to witness the day I ask you to be my wife. My Pops always said this was magical and you and I have referenced that several times over the past few weeks. I believe it because being here brought us back together. We've spent the past few months getting to know each other again, talking about the years we were apart and what we learned from them, but most of all, we've talked about what we want in our future and I know I don't have one that doesn't include you. I want to wake up every morning to tell you I love you and how you make my heart beat. I want to have pretty little babies with you, watching your belly swell with the love we'll create. I want to continue to plan and dream with you and I want to do all of this with you by my side as my wife. I love you, Danielle. Will you marry me?"

By the time Gannon finished talking, she was crying almost hysterically. The man she had loved since she was fifteen years old was asking her to marry him. She looked around and noticed everyone was crying, even her dad. This is how life should have always been, them loving each other with family around. After looking at each person in the room, she turned her attention back to Gannon and through the tears, she shook her head yes.

"Yes. Yes, I will marry you anytime, any day," she said and leaped into his arms, wrapping her legs around his hips, holding on tight as she cried into his shoulder. When she could finally gather herself in the midst of their families clapping and cheering, she leaned back and kissed him with all of the passion she had in her, reserved only for him.

"I love you, baby," he said.

"I love you too."

Epilogue

One year later

The party was in full swing at the lake house. Once again, both families came out for the celebration that would top all celebrations! Gannon raced back and forth in and out of the lake house grabbing more food for the grill. Music blared as family and friends gathered for a good time.

"Gannon, don't forget the hot sauce," Dawn yelled.

Grabbing it, he headed back out to the grill.

"Hot sauce? Really? Don't give any of that to my wife. You'll send her into early labor," Gannon said before leaning down and kissing Danielle in a way she'd come to love. Without notice, at any time, he would kiss her and she was always ready for it.

"She's too early for labor. She's only four months along!" Dawn exclaimed.

"Yeah, well, she loves that stuff and I try to hide it from her. My baby will come out with a love for hot foods!" he shouted as everyone laughed.

"We're celebrating and you know how we love our hot sauce when we party. This is a great day. You and Danielle just graduated from college and that's a major reason to celebrate. More exciting than that is four months after you get married, Danielle is four months pregnant and I can't tell you how excited both families are to hear that."

"I'm more excited than everybody!" Danielle yelled, hearing their conversation.

"Not more than me!" Gannon exclaimed. "You have no idea how long I've wanted to be a father, but I had to wait until the lake brought us back together to put us back on the right path."

"Don't worry baby because this little one is the beginning of many I want to have," Danielle said.

Gannon looked at her and every time he did, he loved her more and more.

"Come take a walk with me," he said and helped her out of the chair she sat in.

"Where are we going?" she asked.

"To the boat."

"The boat? With all the family and friends we have here to celebrate with us?"

"Yes, because I want to be alone with my wife." Gannon placed her arm in his as they walked. The best day of his life happened a few months after he proposed. Neither saw a reason to wait.

Danielle smiled. Gannon made her happy being his love and his wife and she would walk to the ends of the earth with him.

"I can't wait to introduce our children to the lake. There is love, family and happiness here that I want them to experience," she said.

"They will experience that here and in their lives everyday wherever we are. I want to teach them the history of what this lake means to our families and what it means to us. It brought me to you, not once, but twice because we needed this second time to get it right."

"I'm glad we did."

"So am I. This is or lake and it's where our love will forever lead us."

Gannon helped her up on the boat where he wanted to spend the evening on the lake dreaming some more. He once dreamed of a life with Danielle and even though getting to that point took longer than expected, coming back to the lake house where magical things happened was the answer. Now he looked forward to what's next. He'd found his first love on the lake and coming back to the lake, he had found his love again.

House of Cards – The Wingates
Meet the Wingates, heirs to the Charles Laslow fortune.

Jaxson, Essence, Kingston and Asia Wingate had never met their grandfather, one of the richest men in the world. In fact, they didn't know he existed. As children, they were told they didn't have grandparents on their mother's side of the family.

Self-made billionaire, Charles Laslow learned he only had a few months to live and he wanted to spend that time getting to know the only grandchildren he ever had. He had watched them grow and struggle to succeed from a distance. With his riches, he could secure for them their inner most dreams, creating platforms for them to have anything they wanted. The only problem was whether or not his grandchildren could handle their newfound wealth without ruining their lives in the process.

Jack of Hearts – Book 1 of House of Cards

Jaxson Wingate is a struggling singer and musician playing in small clubs for nominal pay. He dreams of a bigger piece of the pie if only he could get one chance to prove what he can do if he had power, money and respect.

Queen of Diamonds – Book 2 of House of Cards

Essence Wingate, worked odd jobs while going to design school in New York City, barely making enough money to cover her monthly rent even with two additional roommates. Unlike most of the students at her school who were leaning toward clothing design, she was more interested in jewelry design. All she needs is one big break to show the most elite stars in the world that she could make them shine as bright as their careers. Barely having two nickels to rub together, she couldn't get close enough to have an audience with anyone who would be willing to give her an opportunity to showcase her exquisite designs. All she needed was one big break.

King of Clubs – Book 3 of House of Cards

Kingston Wingate was tired of his nightclub boss stealing all of his ideas on how to expand his clubs into markets that have so far been untapped. With hundreds of thousands of dollars in college debt, he can't find a way out of working for others when he has an idea that would put him on the map with his own clubs that would draw in the who's who of the entertainment industry. Finding a way to get there was the problem.

Ace of Spades – Book 4 of House of Cards

Asia Montgomery was her parent's greatest disappointment. As the baby of the family, she felt left out and sought love and friendship with the wrong crowd. She never finished anything her parents helped her get on track for, but she learned early that she had a knack for playing cards and winning until she lost, which was usually the result.

After getting caught counting cards at some of the biggest casinos in the world, she knew that she was meant to do and be more. She wanted to find success on the legal side of gambling, but with her record, no one would ever give her a chance. For her, success wasn't about money, power or respect, something her siblings chased. Success in life was about living a life her family would be proud of. Her biggest problem was getting away from those who had always profited from a life that had her looking over her shoulder for the next ball to drop. She needed a chance to prove she was better than that, but didn't know how to get it.

Get the book series, House of Cards – The Wingates, book 1, *Jack of Hearts*, in August 2018.

www.cherylbarton.net

More from Cheryl Barton

Heartthrob

Enjoy this excerpt from *Heartthrob*

"Mr. Weston, can I get a moment of your time?" a voice shouted.

"Cade! Over here please," another voice bellowed in the crowd.

"Cade, what was the most challenging aspect of your most recent film?" a male shouted over all the other voices.

"What do you like most about being Cade Weston? Is it being an actor, running your own record label, having a successful apparel line or the countless number of women who throw themselves at you daily?" a female voice shrieked.

"Can I have your baby?" yelled another.

Cade chuckled. That question he heard almost daily.

"Mr. Weston, what's next for you, is it a new movie or a brand-new business venture?" another voice hollered.

"Mr. Weston, are you single? I have a daughter and I think she'd be perfect for you!"

Cade smiled as questions were being thrown at him from the crowd that gathered outside of the Los Angeles television station. It was daytime, but he had just wrapped up the taping of his appearance on a late-night talk show. He was told to expect the crowd once word got out that he would be there. He expected a crowd, but nothing like what he encountered as he exited the building while his security team made a path to get him into the waiting limousine.

"Cade, what do you think of the nickname everyone has given you, calling you 'Heartthrob'? I hear it's because of the number of broken hearts you leave behind and the throbbing bodies women and some men experience just by getting a glimpse of you?" yet another voice shouted.

Cade stopped in his tracks at hearing himself being called *'Heartthrob'*.

Recently, that pseudonym had been plastered on the cover of every magazine and news story written about him. He liked it, especially when people tried to define the title with their own characterization. He found it hilarious every time he read a new story about him and his sexual prowess, something that kept his name in the headlines.

"You don't have time to stop and answer questions, Cade," Abby, his personal assistant said, urging him to keep walking.

Cade knew she was right and though he was tempted to answer some of them, he continued on to the limousine and got in followed by Abby and Aaron, his chief of security.

"That is some crowd, especially this early in the morning," Aaron said.

Aaron was not only Cade's chief of security, but also one of his best friends since their college days.

"It is and I am who I am because of crowds like that."

"I see this heartthrob thing isn't going away. I'm beginning to believe you're really enjoying the title, brother," Aaron said slyly.

Cade didn't answer, but gave his friend a slick smile. Being labeled a heartthrob and plastered on the cover of magazines certainly had its benefits and he had the bank account and the sex life to prove it.

"I plead the fifth," Cade said with a smirk.

"What's on the agenda for today?" Aaron asked.

"I'm going home to work out and then I believe I have several meetings at the record label. My artists are climbing the charts and because of that, we've been getting in demos from aspiring artists from around the world. There are a few my team, who has the responsibility for finding new talent, want me to hear. Then, later tonight, I'm going to be eye candy on the arm of Ms. Diamond at a fundraising event. Does that about cover it Abby?" he asked turning toward her and making sure he hadn't left anything out. He noticed she had yet to lift her head from her cell phone, no doubt booking him for another public appearance somewhere. He didn't question her; he just followed along with however she planned out his life.

"That's pretty much it. You asked me to clear your

calendar after the event with Ms. Diamond tonight."

Aaron knew what that meant. Cade was often called on to accompany some of the most beautiful women in the world to events to keep the buzz about them in the media and it always worked. He knew that Cade believed that all press was good press in Hollywood. He had, after all, recently been name the sexiest man on the planet. Everyone wanted to be seen with him and all women wanted to get under him, literally. Aaron had a feeling Diamond would be engaging in both before the evening was over.

"Abby, can you get my usual suite ready for tonight and since I'll be entertaining, roll out the usual including my staple gift. Check to be sure it's not one that I've given Diamond in the past."

"Do you want me to add flowers this time as well?" she inquired.

Cade thought about it and knew it wouldn't be necessary with Diamond.

"No flowers tonight, but make sure my driver sticks around since she won't be staying the night."

Abby didn't respond or even react since they were all accustomed to Cade's penchant for entertaining and then moving on. This was going to be one of those nights. He would be doing his part to keep Diamond in the spotlight by being seen with her and in turn, she would spend the evening in whatever way he chose. He was Cade Weston, media mogul, box office smash, actor and of course, according to the everyone in the world who knows anything about him, a *'heartthrob'* and he planned on living up to that name tonight. She loved working for the famous, Cade Weston and she loved that there was never a dull moment.

Get your copy of *Heartthrob* book one of "A Lovers' Heart" book series
at www.cherylbarton.net

Book two of "A Lovers' Heart" book series, *Heartbeat* is now available! Enjoy this excerpt

Heartbeat

Navy SEAL, Calvin Lymon's body purred to life with a desirous hunger unlike anything he had ever experienced before. The word, stunning, streaked like lightning across his mind the moment the statuesque beauty came into his line of sight in the overcrowded pub in the heart of Colombia, South America. The essence of her tantalizing aura radiated so far out from her actual body that everything about her engulfed his very being like a tight embrace that covered him completely.

Calvin couldn't take his eyes away even if he wanted to. Even though the room was packed with patrons from one dusty beige wall to the next, from across the room and through every person that covered the path between them, the woman of his admiring gaze stood out. He watched every scrupulously slow move as she danced and swayed to the Latin music playing loudly through speakers that were place in all four corners of the large, spacious room.

A lump formed in his throat causing him to gulp in disbelief at the immediate impact her loveliness had on him. He had seen and indulged in his share of beautiful women before, but none compared to the woman his eyes were locked on.

Slowly changing the direction of his stare, he looked downward toward the gray and black marbled tiled floor where she stood and his eyes covered her from her brightly painted red toe nails that peaked out at him through strappy white high-heeled stilettos and up her long-toned chestnut brown legs which were visible because of the short white body hugging dress she had on.

From there, he let his eyes continue on their path to hips that flared out, just below her slim waste showcasing her hourglass figure. The way she moved had his mind traveling to a place in time where he imagined himself holding on to all of her curves tightly as her legs wrapped snugly around his hips allowing his body to sink into hers in the most intimate and provocative way. He shifted in his seat as his manhood jumped when his eyes continued an upward path landing on her full, large breasts, the part of a woman that he admired first when it came to the physicality of a sexy woman. His mouth felt as dry as the Mohave desert with a tongue that was as heavy as lead as lascivious thoughts around all he could do with a body like hers flooded through him.

Anxiety overtook him when those in the crowd walking by blocked his view of her as if the very life was being sucked from his body. A sheer moment of disconnect had his heart racing while he stretched his neck as if keeping his eyes on her was what kept his heart beating, giving him life.

Finding an opening, again, the beauty once again came into focus and this time, as she danced, she turned around and he finally got the chance to see her face. To say she was beautiful didn't quite capture the full, powerful punch of her exquisiteness. He had never seen a more perfect woman in his entire life and he had a feeling, he probably never would again. He couldn't focus on anything else other than his life depending on him getting his fill of looking at her.

Her long dark hair flowed down around her shoulders moving in sync with her body's movements. When she raised her hands above her head and slowly swayed down toward the floor, Calvin almost fell off of the chair he'd been sitting on, snapping him briefly out of the trance the beauty had him in.

Remembering to breathe, he looked around and checked to see if anyone else saw what he did and by the look on every guy's face in the pub, he wasn't the only one who noticed her; he wasn't surprised.

A feeling of possession overcame him as he turned his face up in a sneer at every man who looked at her the way he was looking at her. He wanted her, yes, and he assumed every man in the place did as well and he didn't like it one bit. Little did they know that he was Calvin Lymon, Navy SEAL and he had enough confidence to overshadow everyone in the room. This woman was his and there was no way he would lose out on an opportunity to meet her nor would he watch another man spend the night getting to know her the way he was planning to do. No one knew, but she was meant for him.

"You okay, Cal?"

Somewhere in what seemed like a distant place, Calvin heard someone addressing him as Cal, what family and close friends called him, but he couldn't focus on the words because he didn't want to take his attention away from the woman of his dreams. The voice had to be that of Mason, his best friend and fellow Navy SEAL. No one else from their team had accompanied them on their one day off from surveillance in the foreign country. He tried his best to tamper down the intrusion of Mason's voice because it was distracting.

Turning back to the woman who had already stolen his heart, he watched as she moved left and then right until she was again standing tall. The moment she threw her head back and laughed at something, what he didn't know, his libido went off the charts like never before. His body hardened like impenetrable steel.

"Cal, can you hear me?"

He heard the voice again, but didn't want to focus on it just in case the woman in front of him wasn't real, but possibly a mirage. Can any woman really be that beautiful? She was perfection and she would be what a man would call a total package. Everything about her was flawless and the way she carried herself, her magnetism wasn't just externally, but he sensed a strong, confident woman internally, something that meant more to him than what he could see with his eyes.

"Cal? Give me a sign that you hear me?"

Now annoyed that he was being interrupted, he huffed out a response.

"Yes, I can hear you," he said in his head because his mouth wouldn't move. What was wrong with his mouth? He tried again to form words to actually speak, but nothing came out. He could only hear his answer in his head, perhaps due to the loud music wafting out from the speakers.

In an instant, for some reason, the crowd milled back into focus right in front of him, thereby blocking his view of her. He slid down from the stool and tried to find her again as his heart beat sped up and uneasiness put his nerves on edge at the thought that he may have lost his chance because he allowed himself to be distracted by a voice. He didn't want to lose sight of her because he needed to meet her. He needed to tell her that though he'd only set eyes on her for a few minutes, he never wanted to live another day without seeing her beautiful face over and over again.

Calvin wasn't sure he'd actually been living until the moment he'd spotted her. Now, the word, complete, came to mind because that would be the state of his love life if he were able to convince her that they were meant for each other.

"What are you thinking about, Cal?" he heard as he started making his way through the throngs of people who gathered and were now in his way.

Calvin knew he was thinking one thing and one thing only and that was to get to this woman and start a connection he hoped would lead to him showing her that he could be the man of her dreams.

As he pushed his way forward, the crowd seemed to thicken even more as he forced his way through to her. He could hear voices calling out to him and though he wasn't focusing on them, they were familiar. Dismissing them, he didn't want to talk to anyone other than the woman who was the focus of his full attention.

Coming to the point where he thought she had been standing, he couldn't spot her anywhere. Anxiously, he looked around as his heart began to pound in his chest with the thought that she had indeed left and he would never get the chance to talk to her, to get to know her or to let her know that she had such an immediate impact on him that his life would be nothing if he didn't have her in it.

Not seeing her anywhere, he held his head in disappointment as he turned and made his way back toward his seat at the bar. Coming through the crowd, he walked up to the stool, turned and when he looked up, there she was right in front of him and smiling. When she wiggled her finger at him to come closer, he pointed to himself to be sure she was talking to him.

When she nodded yes, he was ecstatic with delight thinking that she must have been watching him as he was watching her and maybe even feeling the connection he'd felt.

As if from a scene in a movie, the crowd parted, clearing a path straight to her. As he began to move in her direction, the smile on her face turned into a frightening frown, one laced with fear and overwrought with terror. He watched as her hand reached up to the side of her neck covering it as her eyes beamed with dread. Looking from her face to where her hand landed, he could see bright red blood begin to seep through her fingers, covering her hand and sliding down to stain the white dress she was wearing. He looked on in horror as she then reached to her stomach where another big red patch of blood began to form and coat the fingers of her other hand. What was happening, he thought as he felt helpless at coming to her aid?

Without thinking, Calvin began running to her, reaching her at the moment when she collapsed to the floor. Holding her in his arms, he could hear her plead with him to help her. He looked around and was stunned to see people were still dancing as if the most beautiful girl in the world was not bleeding to death on the floor right in front of them. He looked for Mason and called out to him for help, but the music was so loud, he knew Mason wouldn't be able to hear him.

Calvin tried to lift her up to get her to a hospital, but her body felt like lead. As her eyes began to close and her hands dropped away, Calvin was puzzled as to what happened. Had she been stabbed? Was it a shooter? He looked around for anything and saw nothing, but crowds of people dancing to the music, laughing and drinking. He tried putting pressure on her neck and then on her side and screamed for anyone to help him. He reached for the person closest to him, but he couldn't get a good grip on his pant leg. His hand, covered in blood seem to go right through the man next to him without even leaving a smear of the blood that now soaked his hand.

Turning back to the woman in his arms, he watched as her body went lifeless while he screamed again for someone, for anyone to help him.

"Cal? Can you hear me? Come on, Cal, calm down. I'm here. Can you hear me?" a voice said.

Calvin struggled to focus on the voice calling out to him. Perhaps that was the help he needed, but the voice he thought he was hearing wouldn't be in Colombia, South America with him. He was on a mission and far away from the glitz and glamour life his brother Cade lived, but he was quite positive that the voice now calling out to him was his Hollywood, superstar brother, Cade Weston. What would Cade be doing in Colombia, he thought? He looked around and didn't see him. Where was he? He tried to speak, but something painful was preventing him from making a sound. His throat felt like it was on fire. It felt blocked with something that was keeping him from speaking.

"Hold on, Cal, the doctor is coming," he heard.

The voice that time was Cameron's, his baby brother who shouldn't be in South America, but in Florida finishing up his last year of his undergraduate program before he started graduate school to continue with his advanced degree in Communications. What was going on? Why are his brothers in South America and why weren't they coming to help him with the dying woman in his arms? He struggled to move and to talk, but could do neither. He felt helpless and weightless as if he was fighting against forces that wanted him to remain still, unable to do anything on his own.

"Mister Lymon, can you hear me? This is doctor Bell. Give me a minute and we'll get the tube out, but I need you to stop struggling with me."

Calvin could feel hands holding him down keeping him from moving.

"Everything's alright, Cal. You're alright, bro."
Cade? That was Cade's voice again, this time a lot closer than before. He wasn't hearing things. How could this be? Cade was in California or Texas or Florida or someplace else with his wife, Callie, but he definitely was not in South America.

"Cal, it's Cam – can you hear me? I'm here, I'm right here. We're all here and you're going to be okay."

Again, he heard Cameron's voice and he knew he must be in the twilight zone. All of a sudden, he felt his body jerk as he struggled to move and breathe. He felt like he was about to regurgitate, but it wasn't quite happening. He couldn't breathe even though he tried with all of his might to do so. Like a man trying to get his last breath, he inhaled and coughed as hard as he could as his eyes suddenly opened. His eyes did a quick, frightening scan and didn't recognize where he was.   What frightened him most was he no longer had the beautiful woman in his arms. Where did she go?

"Breathe easy, Cal. Just breathe easy, bro. That's it."

Being able to see clearly now, he looked around and saw both of his brothers, a guy in a white coat and several other women surrounding him. Where was he?

"Calvin, it's doctor Bell. We took out your breathing tube and it's going to be a few minutes before you'll be able to speak and even then, it will be a strain. Can you look my way? Can you hear me? Do you understand me?"

Calvin couldn't take his eyes from his big brother, Cade. Wherever he was, he felt calmer knowing Cade was there, but he still needed to know why?

"Cade, talk to him. He seems to only want to focus on you," Dr. Bell said.

Cade walked closer to him and Calvin's eyes widened sensing something wasn't quite right.

"Hey, bro. You're woke. I know it's hard to talk and I can see you struggling to do so. The doctor said it's going to be hard, so just nod if you can understand me. Nod, Cal," Cade said sternly.

Shifting his eyes to the left he saw that standing next to Cade was Cameron who was also encouraging him to remain calm. Something was wrong if both of his brothers were standing over him and a doctor was talking to him. Was he in a bed?

Doing what Cade asked, he nodded. He looked to Cameron who cheered with excitement, no longer with a worried facial expression.

Calvin couldn't get his thoughts to line up to explain what was going on. One moment he was back in the bar with Sofia and then all of a sudden, she began bleeding from wounds and he couldn't help her. Sofia? Where was she? He already knew her name? Why was she bleeding like that on the day that they'd met which had been over a year ago? Was that right? He was so confused.

As his thoughts began to clear and the voices around him began to converse with each other, he thought back to a moment ago when he'd held Sofia's lifeless body in his arms. He couldn't make sense of the scene that had played out. Sofia hadn't died in his arms in the pub and not on the day that they'd met. Now that his memory was clearing up, he remembered that she may not have died in his arms in the pub, but she had died and remembered seeing her body and being overwhelmed with grief.

He now knew that for a year and a half, he and Sofia had been in love and then it all ended the day she died. She was gone and the thought startled him. Something else was wrong as a sudden pain pierced his heart. They have a son! He and Sofia have a son and his name is Camico. Where was Camico? Sofia was dead, but where was their son? He'd promised her he'd look after Camico, but where was he? If he was in a hospital or some facility where his brothers were and doctors and nurses were tending to him, where was his son? A feeling of trepidation overtook him as he tried with all of his might to form the words. With everything in him, he screamed at the top of his lungs.

"Camico!"

Everyone in the room turned toward him. Before he could decipher what was happening, where he was and when, the room went completely dark. Calvin had passed out.

Get your copy of *Heartbeat*, book two of "A Lovers' Heart" book series at www.cherylbarton.net

Coming up next from "A Lovers' Heart" book
series, *Heartbreaker,*
Cameron Lymon's story.

Cameron Lymon if fresh out of college with his Master's degree in Journalism with a minor in Communications and Sports Management and has landed a job that has never been offered to someone fresh out of school. Heading off to Denver, Colorado to start his career as the co-anchor for a new morning show, he isn't prepared for the steamy encounters with his co-host ten years older than him and fifty shades hot. What started as casual hookups, soon leads to more than just clandestine rendezvous around the station. Cameron was losing his heart and his playboy status for a woman who showed him how to stop playing at love and just love.

Cameron's story is coming to you in late 2018.

The Bachelor Series

Book 1 - *Bachelor Not for Sale* – Now available

Duron Knight agreed to take part in a bachelor auction held by his sister's sorority. Little did he know that he would find the woman of his dreams in the form of sexy bombshell Taija Charles, the woman in red.

Taija, in a room full of the sexiest men in Atlanta, has eyes for one handsome bachelor that no woman in her right mind could resist.

As sparks fly between them, can Duron put his unhappy past with women behind him and give his all to Taija? He may fight love, but Taija has plans to help him mend his broken heart with real love and a whole lot of lust.

Book 2 – *A Designed Affair* – Now available

In this follow-up to "Bachelor Not for Sale", Loren Knight has been engaging in a secret love affair with her brother Duron's best friend and business partner, Michael Bailey. He is everything she could want and more in a man, but she believes the risk is too great for any type of relationship with him beyond their steamy encounters behind closed doors.

Michael Bailey has been fighting his attraction to Loren for years. He has stayed away from her out of respect for his best friend and business partner. Now that he and Loren have finally given into the passion they have been craving, can Michael convince Loren that what they share is worth the risk of even Duron finding out?

Book 3 – *A Perfect Combination* – Now available

In this second follow-up to "Bachelor Not for Sale", Tyrone Davis is the king of one-night stands. The nickname, *Mr. Love'em* and *Leave'em*, given to him in his college days, still follows him as a top executive in the corporate world. He never believed in karma until it paid him a visit in the form of a very sexy and uninhibited one-night stand.

Victoria Alston couldn't forget the incredible night she spent with Tyrone Davis, someone connected to her best friends. In just one night, he stirred feelings in her she never thought she would ever experience. The next day, she disappeared, returning to reality and the fiancé she left back in Boston.

Tyrone and Victoria both soon discover that it wasn't just a one-night stand, but a perfect combination for the kind of love most people only dream about.

Book 4 – *Love at Last* – Now available

They had the perfect love…That's what Brian Knight thought of his relationship with Sherry

Braxton until he looked up one day and she was gone and never wanted to see him again.

Two years later, he discovered that there is the possibility that Sherry may have been pregnant with his child. Hurt and angry at her deceit, he takes a flight to Baltimore to fight for his rights as a father and realizes that the love and passion they once shared had never died.

Is it possible he could still have the kind of love he thought would last a lifetime? Can he still have his love at last?

About the Author

Cheryl Barton lives in Maryland and in her spare time she loves to read espionage novels, cook, watch Sci-fi movies, spend time with family and friends and enjoy Maryland steamed crabs.

Indulge in more romance and inspirational novels by visiting her website at www.cherylbarton.net.

Cheryl is a member of the Romance Writers of America – National Chapter and the Maryland Romance Writers.

Connect with me

Visit my website at www.CherylBarton.net
Twitter – @Author Cheryl Barton
Instagram – AuthorCherylBarton
Facebook at Author Cheryl Barton
Email – Cheryl@CherylBarton.net
Blog - https://mswriterinmd.wordpress.com/
Publisher website – www.crbarton.com

www.ingramcontent.com/pod-product-compliance
Lightning Source LLC
Chambersburg PA
CBHW021014180626
46814CB00003B/1275